Under the Clock

THE NETTLEBY TRILOGY - BOOK TWO

ROSIE CHAPEL

ULFIRE PTY LTD

First printing 2022
ISBN (E-book): 978-0-6454794-6-1
ISBN (Print): 978-0-6454794-7-8

Ulfire Pty. Ltd.
P.O. Box 1481
South Perth
WA 6951
Australia

www.rosiechapel.com

Cover Design: Lisa Miller with Got You Covered.

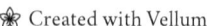 Created with Vellum

Acknowledgments

Thank you to…

Joseph and Eliza Elliott, without whom this trilogy would not exist. I wish I had known them but am proud a little of their blood runs in my veins.

Mum, for proofing this manuscript.

Nick for his generous help with military details.

Graham, my very patient editor from *A Fading Street Publishing*.

Melanie, for being my sounding board.

My awesome husband - just because.

Under the Clock

The Nettleby Trilogy - Book Two

A WWI Novella

Prologue

December 1916 – Brigg Station
Maisie

I was standing under the clock. It was a frigid day: the sky was leaden, frost clung to the trees, and a covering of snow carpeted the ground.

Thank goodness, the track was clear… *please let there be no delays.*

I stamped my feet, trying to stay warm. The dark grey of my winter coat alleviated — in honour of this very special occasion — by a splash of colour in the form of my new hat.

Although soft, the dusky pink material resembled a fine straw weave. Broad brimmed, it was trimmed with a kind of rolled band and a stylish bow, through which a jaunty faux feather in the same delicate hue was threaded.

A totally frivolous accessory, and utterly useless in this weather, but I loved it. It was similar to the one I wore the first time Fred invited me to share a pot of tea, the day my life changed... and I hoped he would remember.

At least the scarf I had bought to go with it was proving worth the exorbitant price.

Maintaining my poise was an effort when all I wanted to do was sing and shout and skip along the platform... *always so ladylike, Maisie.* Instead of giving in to the urge and behaving like a hoyden, I tried, by way of distraction, to coerce my thoughts down a different tack.

That lasted less than two shakes of a lamb's tail, my mind veering back to Fred.

I kept glancing at the clock... *had the hands moved at all?* It felt as though I had waited half my life for this moment. In fact, it was only two years but, under the circumstances, a lifetime would seem shorter. I had been counting the days since I received his letter telling me he was coming home.

Had he changed? Had he lost that sweet smile? Would he recognise me. I was struck by a nerve-wracking thought. *Would I recognise him?* Fred had been gone for so long; endless months during which he had witnessed untold horrors and lost many of his friends.

Unbidden, I remembered when Joe Elliott returned after being declared missing presumed dead. Husband of my best friend, Lizzie, Joe was pinched and drawn, but I had no difficulty recognising him, despite the fact I thought he was a ghost.

A wry smile played around my mouth in recollection of that scene.

It was well over a year since Joe had been discharged. Hundreds... no... more like thousands of families would never hear those words, and I thanked the Lord, I numbered among the fortunate few whose loved one had survived.

I conjured up Fred in my mind's eye.

Tall and brawny with an upright stance, unruly dark hair,

twinkling brown eyes, and hands which resembled spades but could work on the finest of projects.

Never had a uniform looked as good as it did on my Fred — of course, I might have been biased.

The curious tremors rippling through me steadied.

I would know Fred anywhere.

Several people greeted me as they sought their vantage point. Happy faces testament to their excitement for a homecoming most thought improbable at best.

The news filtering through from the front was hardly encouraging. Those on the train might have escaped the trenches, but it was doubtful they had shed the shackles of war, given they had been sent home after being wounded.

Like my Fred, like Joe.

My husband had been shot during the Battle of Albert, the opening salvo of what the papers referred to as the Somme Offensive. The courage shown by his regiment, duly recognised by their superiors. Several, Fred among them, had been granted the Military Medal.

I had imagined his reaction to being singled out for mention. Essentially an unassuming, reserved man, he would deem others more deserving of the merit than he and, if one was worthy of a commendation... they all were.

Through carefully worded letters, all I managed to glean was that his division had moved several times over the past year, including... if I could trust what I had deciphered... a brief stint in Egypt. *Egypt...* I still struggled to comprehend that, and speculated whether I had misunderstood, that was a deliberate ploy to fool the censors.

Even so, I had no idea Fred was anywhere near the

Somme until weeks after the fact. I'm sure, said censors would be delighted to know their efforts, in that regard, had proved successful.

Among my grandmother's books was a beautiful atlas, incredibly detailed, and I found the Somme, a river which ran 152 miles from somewhere called Fonsommes to the Channel. I had scoured its meandering length, trying to picture where Fred might be stationed.

Examined at the front, Fred was transported to a field hospital by, of all people, Polly who, along with Lizzie and me, made up a tight-knit friendship. A trio closer than some families.

Six months prior to Fred being injured, Polly — already training to be a nurse — announced her intention to volunteer for the military hospitals, with the aim of becoming one of the ambulance drivers.

Deranged does not begin to describe her scheme, but she refused to be dissuaded, and I got a shock when I realised she was within range of Fred's unit.

Polly wrote to me, long before Fred was able to — although she had been kind enough to pen one on his behalf — explaining what led up to his hospitalisation, and assuring me his injuries were not life-threatening.

That was good and bad. Good, in that he wasn't grievously hurt. Bad because this meant he would return to the front.

Upon his release from the hospital, he was granted leave, but chose not to come home; most of it would be wasted travelling.

I was upset and relieved.

To see him, to hold him, to feel his lips on mine was all I

dreamt about, but to have that snatched away almost imme-diately would have broken my heart.

Two weeks ago, a letter arrived. Fred was being demobilised. His damaged shoulder had not healed properly, leaving him unable to perform his military duties.

He was frustratingly brief, leaving me with more ques-tions than answers.

Details, Fred. Details. Did he not realise I would be worried sick? *Unable to perform his military duties* — what did that mean?

I had to force myself not to dwell on it, because each scenario was more gruesome than the last. The only thing I could do was hope for the best, prepare for the worst, then wait and see.

Two more letters followed, but they related to his travel arrangements rather than the reason he was being sent home.

Polly had said it was a shoulder injury, sustained when carrying the wounded out of no man's land. The swell of pride I experienced whenever I pondered his valour, suffused me.

It was an emotion I kept to myself, not conceited or insensitive enough to voice it, but nothing could change the fact, my Fred was a bloody hero — the expletive, entirely justified.

I spied the puff of steam in the distance and long-suppressed anticipation began to bubble up.

People crowded the platform. Most, like me, were there to welcome home a loved one.

I stayed where I was.
Fred knew where to find me.
It was our special place — under the clock.

Out of the corner of my eye, I caught sight of a young girl tending to the flowers in front of the little shop on the station concourse.

The shop where I used to work.
The place I met Fred.
Before I could stop them, memories flooded in.

One

June 1908 – Brigg Station, Lincolnshire
Maisie

Every Friday, at precisely five to six, a young man arrives on the platform. I know the time because I can see the clock.

Five minutes later, the train pulls in, punctual as always.

Among the alighting passengers, an elderly gentleman. The young man greets him with a smile and a handshake, then tucks his arm through the older man's and they leave the station.

Every Friday.

The young man is tall, broad, and jovial. He has dark brown hair, chestnut almost, and I like to think his eyes are hazel, but we have never been close enough for me to know for sure.

I estimated his age to be around twenty-two or three, which made him a year or so older than me, but I could be completely wrong. I am not very good at guessing people's ages.

I had overheard the elderly chap call his companion, Fred. I liked that name, it suited him. A steady name, a reliable name, the name of someone you could trust.

Without fail, he tips his cap to me, and one afternoon, he bought a bouquet from my stall. I supposed it was for his wife or his girl, ignoring the tinge of sadness that caused.

It was a ridiculous sentiment. How could I feel *anything*? We were strangers, two people who had become part of each other's lives through routine. Once a week we shared a glance or two and, to be fair, I suspect I noticed him more than he noticed me.

The flower shop where I work, afforded me the perfect position to watch the comings and goings at our little station on the Grimsby branch line.

The people who use the train had become as familiar as my own family. I often talked to the passengers as they arrived or departed, cheerful flurries of gossip breaking up the monotony of my days.

I invented scenarios, ways for Fred and I to extend our brief encounters, but was never quite able to come up with a topic of conversation which didn't sound banal or contrived.

So, we smiled — he has the most wonderful smile, it makes my heart miss a beat... or three — nodded, and exchanged the occasional hello.

I hoped the bouquet *wasn't* for his wife or rather, and more importantly, I hoped Fred didn't have a wife.

A vain hope maybe, but I'm allowed to dream.

June 1908 – Brigg Station
Fred

I count the hours until Friday afternoon comes around. Not only because this marks the start of the weekend but also, and more importantly, I get to see the flower girl.

I am clueless as to her name, yet my heart begins to race the minute the station comes into view. I almost run up the steps onto the platform, hoping for a glimpse of her bright smile.

I doubt she ever notices me. I'm just a village lad, come to meet my grandpa.

She must see so many people every day, I was one more faceless person in the throng.

One day, I bought a bouquet, just to speak to her. I suffered Mam telling me I was daft, wasting my hard-earned wage on flowers when I handed them to her — Dad rarely made such extravagant gestures — but it was worth it.

I might not know her name, but I *do* know she has glossy brown hair. There's always a loose ringlet framing her face in spite of her attempts to restrain it in... what do ladies call it... a bun, I think. I imagined removing the pins from that bun, watching it unwind over her shoulders, and entangling my fingers in those shining curls.

Her attire hints at a subtle rebellion, which I find intriguing. By chance, while waiting for grandpa, I caught a flash of bare arm where a sleeve ought to be and, although no aficionado of women's fashion, it puzzled me. Her garments are invariably sober... grey, brown, or black... in keeping with her job, save this sole and somewhat radical inconsistency.

Oh, to peel back her layers.

The conundrum was solved when, on another occasion, just as the train chugged to a standstill, I happened to spy her tweaking a wisp of black lace from under the cuff of her blouse, the gauzy material falling to her elbows.

I felt a grin forming at her artful subterfuge and applauded her practicality, presumably precipitated after suffering the daily discomfort of wet material sticking to her. An inevitable consequence of continually plucking flowers from pails of cold water.

Her enterprising nature and tacit defiance merely added to her appeal.

Given she was working at the flower shop, I clung, obstinately, to the belief she was not yet wed... furnishing me with a modicum of hope... however absurd.

In truth, I reckoned she was being courted by some handsome, eligible, and undoubtedly wealthy, bachelor who had much more to offer than I. *She was so beautiful; how could this not be the case?*

To my annoyance, a picture of this imaginary beau had formed in my head.

He would speak in cultured tones, look down his nose at the likes of me, have his clothes tailor-made in London, probably owned a car, and a mansion. I hated him with a passion.

My origins are far more humble. My family owns the shop, which also houses the post office, in the tiny village of Nettleby-under-Wold, and I work as a farmhand.

I was under no illusions about my suitability. I wasn't anyone's idea of a catch — ignoring the slight pinch in my chest — but I was allowed to dream.

· · ·

If I arrived early, I would wait under the clock. It was a bit of a feature… I think it had been presented to the station by a local bigwig years ago.

Some folk thought it a frivolous addition, but I rather liked it. The wrought iron housing, although quite ornate, complemented the splendid red-brick station with its lofty arches, white eaves and glass canopies.

Black Roman numerals and the finely crafted hands set against a white background, were clearly visible from one end of the platform to the other… and much easier to read than most station clocks. The slender pedestal rose to support elaborate swirls on top of which the circular face balanced effortlessly.

A curved stone bench was tucked beneath it, but I never took advantage, preferring to lean against the post, which felt less like I was loitering. The clock's position on the platform allowed me to observe the flower girl serving her customers, without seeming to.

Eventually, I plucked up the courage to mutter a 'hello'. What I really wanted was to invite her out for afternoon tea, or a walk, but each time I tried, the words stuck in my throat and that pathetic greeting was all I accomplished.

One day…

Two

June 1908 – Brigg Station
Maisie

I t had been a very long week. I loved my job, but the owner was on holiday, leaving me twice as busy as usual and the days seemed endless.

There at 6 a.m. for the flower delivery, by the time I had tidied up and tallied the day's takings, 6 p.m. had become a distant memory. It was all I could do to get home, eat a quick supper, and fall into bed.

Thank goodness it was Friday afternoon. My back ached, my feet ached, even my eyes ached. I wanted nothing more than to be in my comfortable abode, with my feet up, nursing a good strong cup of tea, or better still — a sherry.

Glancing at the clock on the platform, I saw it was coming up on five to six. My heart did an odd flutter. *Seriously Maisie*, I admonished internally, *you are like a giddy girl, not a sensible working woman on the cusp of her majority.*

Simultaneously, wheels crunched on the gravel outside. They sounded more like a bike than a horse and cart... *perhaps Fred wasn't coming today... but it was Friday.*

Stubbornly optimistic, I tidied my hair. A pointless exercise because it had a mind of its own and by day's end was unravelling from the bun into which it had been twisted. I tried to capture the errant strands with pins, but probably made it worse.

Running my hands over my pinafore to smooth any wrinkles, I swallowed, striving to appear dignified, respectable, and friendly. A wasted effort because I completely forgot to unfurl my sleeves, which I tended to tuck out of the way while handling the flowers. It was a habit I had developed to prevent the flimsy lace getting wet and sticking to me — a disagreeable sensation — and worth the odd raised brow.

All this for the possibility of a nod or a smile, *pathetic Maisie.*

The train pulled in and people tumbled out, some chattering together, some in solitary contemplation. All looked weary, and I wondered where they had been.

Creating fictitious lives for people I didn't know, allayed the tedium when the shop was quiet. I invented an occupation, a home, husbands, wives, children, possibly a dog. A spy, a politician, a military man wearing civilian clothes. A lady of the aristocracy disguised as a maid, or vice versa.

I could be engrossed for hours, but no one consumed my thoughts more than Fred. I feared I was becoming obsessed. His face popped into my head at random intervals and with increasing frequency.

The recollection of his smile made my heart trip, and I longed to hear his voice — that lovely deep voice — just once, on a Friday afternoon.

I forced myself to concentrate on the passing travellers. There were still several bunches of flowers left, and they presented a vivid array in the summer sunlight. A young woman bought a posy, grateful when I assured her they were half price.

A large hand scooped up the remaining flowers.

Astonished, my gaze slid upwards.

It was Fred.

Of the older gentleman, there was no sign.

"How much?" he asked, a broad grin on his tanned face.

"Sir, that's a lot of flowers."

"I know." He didn't replace them, and his expression told me, he intended to buy them whatever the cost.

I stared at him, dubiously. "I could give you them for a shilling." Embarrassed at how expensive that sounded. They were just flowers.

"Cheap at half the price."

"Here, let me wrap them for you." I reached out to take the blooms from him, and my hand grazed his. A tingle spiralled up my arm. I froze. *Had he felt it too?*

Our eyes met and held. I fought to suppress a smile when I noticed his were a velvety, dark brown… *so much for hazel.* Once seen, I could not imagine them being any other colour.

I coerced my wayward brain back to the matter at hand. Fred was watching me, clearly amused.

"Forgive me, I… err…" I stuttered. *What plausible excuse could I offer? 'I am sorry, sir. I was drowning in your beautiful eyes.' Probably not the best thing to say to a complete stranger and a man to boot.*

"Naught to fret about. I'm Fred Cuthbert by the way." The lift in his tone invited me to reciprocate.

"I know… well… I know you are Fred, not the Cuthbert part…" *Good grief, Maisie what is* wrong *with you.* I lowered my gaze as heat washed up my cheeks, and prayed for the ground to swallow me whole, or that I could turn back the clock to start this conversation all over again.

"And you are?" His expectant question snapped my eyes back to his.

"I'm Maisie Vickers," I replied, unaccountably shy... a first for me. In my job, one must be gregarious, be comfortable talking to people from every station of life, yet all of a sudden, I was tongue-tied.

"It is a great pleasure to meet you, Miss Maisie Vickers," he paused, then added delicately, "it is Miss?"

I blushed again... *honestly, talk about hopeless*. "Likewise, and yes." Was the best I could come up with. Internally berating myself at my lack of sophistication, I took refuge in wrapping the flowers.

After tying a length of red ribbon in a large bow around the brown paper, I handed them over, ignoring that same sense of desolation at the knowledge the bouquet was probably for his girl. "That'll be a shilling."

He accepted the flowers, dropping a sixpence and two thruppenny bits onto the counter in payment.

He took five steps, then spun on his heels and, with a purposeful stride, returned to my side.

I raised a puzzled brow. *Did I owe him some change? No, he gave me the correct amount.*

"I wonder, may I be so bold as to ask whether you might be kind enough to join me for a pot of tea across the way?" He nodded through the arch of the station entrance towards the café at the other side of the street. A favourite haunt on a Friday evening because it stayed open until eight. *Eight... the decadence.*

"Y-your... the elderly gentleman?" I stammered.

"Is not coming this evening."

"Then why...?" Perplexed, I stared at him.

It was his turn to flush and he fidgeted uncomfortably. "I came to see you," he blurted out.

"B-beg pardon?" I quizzed, positive I was hearing things. *To see me? Did he really just say to see me? Oh my goodness.*

I watched him heave what I assumed to be a steadying breath.

"To see you."

This time there was no doubt.

"M-me?" My heart hiccupped and I knew I must look like a gawking fool, but for the life of me I could not get my brain and my mouth to cooperate.

He dipped his head, smiled, and repeated his request, "Please grant me the honour of accompanying me for a spot of tea."

"I need to…" Fighting the urge to fan my face at his chivalrous turn of phrase, I swung my arm, encompassing the various buckets and the wooden barrow which made up the display at the front of the little shop.

"Permit me to assist, that way you will be done more quickly."

My mouth opened and closed; a reply refused to form. Finally, I marshalled my senses, gave a jerky nod and, mechanically, began the end of business routine.

Fred emptied the water out of the buckets and stacked them on the barrow which he wheeled into the shop at my direction. Faster than I have ever done before, I recorded the takings, checked everything was as it should be, and dropped the blinds. At the last minute, I remembered to unroll my sleeves, pinned on my hat — glad I was wearing my favourite one — lifted my shawl from its hook, and locked up.

"Miss Vickers." Fred offered his arm.

After a brief hesitation, I accepted, and he escorted me through the station concourse and across the road.

Three

June 1908 – Brigg Station
Fred

I can't believe I had the audacity to ask her out. Not only that, but also, she said yes. I know it's just a cup of tea, but I did it, and she accepted.

I wanted to shout my success to the sky but reined in my exuberance. No need to scare her off before we've had a proper conversation.

Maisie locked the door of the shop and turned. To my abject disappointment, while gathering her belongings, she had released her sleeves from their confines. The lace effectively veiled her satiny skin, and I itched to reverse the gesture.

Perched on her dark curls at a rakish angle, a hat in some impossible shade of pink and, although looked too dainty for every day wear, the style suited her. The shawl slung around her shoulders, matched her hat, the vibrant colour — a striking foil to the sedate black and grey of her outfit — seemed to enhance the sparkle in her beautiful eyes.

Her eyes… fleetingly, my thoughts wandered off on *the* most delightful path but, with effort, I steered them back to the moment, and offered my arm.

Her hand on my shirt sent warmth snaking along my veins, the sensation both thrilling and unnerving. Since first I clapped eyes on her, I knew there was something special about Miss Maisie Vickers, something my subconscious told me was worth nurturing.

I sounded like a lovelorn schoolboy, not the almost twenty-two-year-old, no-nonsense labourer I really was, but the notion refused to be banished. I have courted the odd girl from the village — who of my age hasn't? — but neither of them made my heart pound the way Maisie does.

If I had my way, I would spend a large portion of each day sitting on the stone bench under the clock on the platform, watching Maisie sell flowers, or jump on my bicycle after work and pedal like the dickens to buy her last posy.

It is not enough to see her smile once a week, I want to see it all the time.

We were shown to a table at the rear of the café overlooking the pretty garden. It was a trifle secluded and, given we were not husband and wife or even a courting couple, I hesitated.

"Fred?" Maisie's voice penetrated my thoughts.

"We can ask for another table if you prefer…"

"Why? What's wrong with this one? We can talk without being overheard and the view is much nicer than at the front. I get a surfeit of the station during the day." She grinned engagingly and my anxiety dissipated.

I ordered the special, which comprised a pot of tea for

two and a plate of toasted teacakes dripping with butter. The savoury aroma made my mouth water.

After a brief and vaguely awkward silence, we both spoke at once. That made us laugh, diffusing any lingering tension, and we began to chat quite naturally.

I discovered Maisie had worked at the flower shop for three years, and lived in her grandmother's house in Wrawby, which she had inherited along with a grumpy cat called Mittens, and Pete, a garrulous bird.

"Your parents?" I dared to pry.

"Live in Nottingham, along with my younger brother and sister."

"Do you miss them?"

She pondered this, her nose crinkling in thought, and it was all I could do not to lean over the table to kiss the pert tip.

"Sometimes," she conceded. "When I have had a long day or a customer has complained about something I have no control over, it would be nice to talk to them, to be able to vent my frustration. Thankfully, those instances are rare." She shrugged philosophically. "I try to visit at least once a month and do love spending time with them, but I also cherish having my own home."

A curious note in her reply prompted me to quirk an enquiring brow.

Her mouth curved in a half-smile. "They do not like me living alone, so far from them. My parents are wonderful, but they belong to a different world. I cannot recall the last time they ventured beyond the boundary of the town. Their lives revolve around the house, the allotment, and church."

"How do your brother and sister fare?"

"Elsie wants to come and live with me, but she's only fifteen. My mother would never permit it, and neither do I want that responsibility. She, Elsie, is enamoured of Florence

Nightingale and wants to become a nurse, so she would be better served staying in Nottingham; both the Bagthorpe and the General offer training." She named the two hospitals in the city.

"As for Colin, he rambles through life without a care. That said, he *is* fascinated by aviation, which might prove the encouragement he needs to pursue his studies with a little more dedication." She rolled her eyes expressively. "Now it's your turn."

"Hmmm… not very exciting, I'm afraid. I live in Nettleby-under-Wold. I am an only child, and my parents own the village shop."

"Oh, I know your shop," she gave a delighted squeak. "I have stopped in on occasion. Do you help out?"

Impressed she had *heard* of the village, let alone was familiar with it, I swallowed a bark of laughter.

"Not on your life. Working for my parents would end badly. I love them, but in their eyes, I am still a child. They stand at my shoulder when I stack the shelves, ready to pounce if one of the tins is not correctly aligned. If I jot down an order, they double check it, and heaven help me if I am five minutes late with the mail."

I looked down at my hands, then back up at Maisie. "No, I'm a labourer on Elliotts' farm. 'Tis long hours and back-breaking but rewarding all the same."

"How lucky to spend your days in the fresh air."

"Not much fun in the rain or snow, or when the sun's beating down on you." I grimaced.

"I suppose so, but whatever the season, I prefer being out to in. Yon wolds are my favourite place to explore, there is something quite magical about them." She tilted her head, and a dreamy smile painted her lovely features.

If I wasn't already half-way in love with Maisie, *this* would have kindled my affection, and explained how she knew of Nettleby. "I agree, but it is unusual to hear them lauded by a city lady."

"City lady? Get away with you. Maybe once upon a time, but not anymore. I am a convert to the quiet life of a country village." Her riposte was accompanied by a slight jut of her chin, almost a challenge.

Chuckling, I raised my palms. "Fine, fine, I will never refer to you as a city lady again."

"I should think not… city lady," she tsked, the humour in her voice belying her affront.

I leant back in the chair, the better to study her. She was exquisite, there was no denying it. Creamy skin, ever-so-slightly tip tilted nose, and sensuous mouth. My heart rate increased as I imagined grazing my thumb over her bottom lip, or better still kissing her slowly, and leisurely, while stroking her slender throat all the way down to the neckline of her blouse.

Shocked at the direction of my thoughts, I lifted my gaze, to see her blue-grey eyes — such a contrast with her dark hair and framed by sooty lashes — contemplating me quizzically.

"I cannot help myself," I apologised with a self-deprecating gesture. "You take my breath away."

She wagged a finger at me. "Mr Cuthbert, for shame, you are outrageous. Wait… don't tell me… are you the Don Juan of Nettleby-under-Wold?"

I stared at her in confusion then, grasped her inference and burst out laughing. "Oh, if only I had his eloquence, good looks, and suave sophistication." I sobered and reached across to place my hand on top of hers resting on the pristine white tablecloth. "I am not flirting."

A faint pink swept up her cheeks, and she dipped her head but did not remove her hand. "Might you be so kind as to elaborate?" she asked.

I considered my words carefully. I wanted to divulge the depth of my regard without scaring her away.

"I do believe we share a rapport, dare I say attraction, one I should like to extend, if you are willing."

I heard a swift intake of breath. Turning Maisie's hand, I traced her palm and along her fingers, until only the tips touched. "I know I am only a humble farm labourer, but I promise to treat you like a princess."

Four

Maisie

The tearoom, along with clink of crockery and gossip of the other patrons, receded as his words washed over me.

A nebulous warning clanged at the back of my brain. *He sounds too good to be true. Was he sincere? Could I trust him? Treat me like a princess? Who speaks like that nowadays?*

My reply got lodged in my throat. *Humble? Good gracious, there is nothing humble about you, Mr Fred Cuthbert.*

I closed my eyes, hoping to steady my thoughts. It didn't work. When I opened them, he was watching me anxiously. I noticed a hint of red creeping up his cheeks and a tightly clenched jaw. He was on edge. Telling in itself. Relief stifled my qualms, and I relaxed.

"A princess you say? Well, good sir, you have my undivided attention, pray, do go on," I managed nonchalantly.

His eyes widened, he released a long breath, and his

mouth curved into the sweetest smile, which did funny things to my insides.

"Hmmm." He tapped his chin and twinkled across the table at me. "You will have to wait and see."

Right then, it happened.

I blinked, aware that somehow, I was already lost, had been since the day I first saw him. It had just taken my head until now to catch up to my heart.

I pushed that to one side, determined not to look like a simpering fool, and we fell back into easy chitchat.

Fred did not relinquish my hand. His fingers played over mine, almost absently, eliciting that same tingle. It was quite the headiest sensation.

I never wanted him to stop.

Fred

I don't think I had ever held my breath for so long. Mind, never did I have so much riding on an answer before. For a while, I thought I had overstated my case, especially as when I got nervous, I tended to trip over my tongue. She was going to rebuff me, of that I was certain.

She did not.

As we resumed our conversation, I caught a glimmer of a profound emotion dancing in her eyes. It mirrored something deep inside me.

The afternoon went from entertaining to enchanting.

We talked about all manner of subjects, and discovered we had more in common than an appreciation of the wolds. History, books, and music, to name a few... although the latter was more a case of I knew what I liked, rather than any detailed knowledge of composers or their works.

Maisie revealed books were her weakness, gratified her grandmother had been of a similar disposition.

"I have too many." She chuckled. "There are bookshelves in every room, even the kitchen. Grandmama was a bit of a hoarder and owned some dating back decades. I should be glad to show you them one day."

One day.

Two words. On their own quite innocuous but, in this context, pivotal. They meant Maisie was already thinking in terms of 'us', however unconsciously, and it took all my self-control to repress the silly grin threatening to split my face.

Too soon, it was time to part. We stepped out of the café into the mellow light of the evening. The balmy air was filled with the sonorous drone of insects and the excited trill of the birds chasing after them. Lincolnshire in summer was very special.

"Do you have any free time at weekends?" I asked.

"Except for church on Sunday morning, I am as free as a bird," Maisie replied.

"Would you like to take a walk with me tomorrow, if you have no prior engagements?" I invited before my brain talked me out of it.

Formality seemed to have supplanted our cheery banter, and I had no idea how to recapture it. As Maisie lived alone, I could not observe the normal rules of courtship, but propriety had its place.

Even though we had enjoyed an impromptu evening, it was customary for a gentleman to call on a lady *before* any outings were arranged.

While accepting my approach was very much cart before

the horse, I hoped my suggestion skirted around the rules without breaking them.

"That sounds lovely," she beamed up at me, and just like that, I lost my heart. In truth, I lost it weeks ago, I simply did not have the wit to recognise it.

Mam narrowed her eyes at me over the profusion of flowers. "Frederick James Cuthbert, who is she?"

"I… errr… what do you mean?" Fiery colour stained my face right up to my hairline.

"Flowers… again, and you are late. You must think me addled if you expect me to believe this is because you love your old Mam."

"Well, I do." I took a step backwards.

Her tone gentled. "I know you do, and thank you for these, but surely asking whether you might call on her would be cheaper than buying all her flowers every Friday. I assume she's the florist's lass at the station?"

I gaped at her.

"I was young once," she winked, "and I know how men think."

Thus, it began. I continued to meet my grandpa off the Friday afternoon train, but now made it my mission to arrive at least fifteen minutes early, so I could stand under the clock on the platform and watch Maisie.

As I had before I mustered up the courage to ask her to tea, I propped myself against the post, and made every effort to appear as though I was doing nothing more than waiting for the train… *not* admiring Maisie.

Except, of course, she knew I was there.

She took to bringing me a cup of tea, which led to a stolen kiss or three — her blushes were quite the most delightful sight.

I took to calling her my flower girl, which led to a furrowed brow... feigned, I could tell... and more kisses.

My grand scheme to take things gradually was ruined because I had no patience and, following that evening, we seized every opportunity to meet.

It was an idyllic summer, the weather was glorious, the days were long and sunny but not too hot. Our weekends were filled with walks and picnics, train rides and afternoon teas.

She introduced me to her family, and I did the same, neither of us particularly surprised by the reserved reactions from both sides.

By August, I knew I was going to propose before the harvest was gathered in.

"Be careful, Fred," my best friend, Joe, cautioned. He was sitting against a hedge chewing a grass stalk one afternoon while we took a break. "Does Maisie feel the same way? You hardly know each other. You've only been courting a couple of months."

"When did you know you loved Lizzie?" I deflected, referring to his girl who had won Joe's heart years ago. The day before her ninth birthday when she took a nasty tumble.

Joe had helped her up, mopping her scuffed knees as well as her tears, while I fetched her Dad. Lizzie told him he was gallant and when she smiled at him, something changed. A subtle ripple in awareness so tenuous, it was imperceptible to anyone who hadn't witnessed it.

Of course, Joe didn't realise it at the time, neither of us did — he was only thirteen and would have scoffed at the mere suggestion of anything deeper than friendship — but I swear that was the day Lizzie stole his heart.

I used to tease him about how devoted he was, the pair of them were barely more than kids. Now I understood.

Joe lifted his hands in surrender. "Fair enough," he acceded. "I just don't want you getting burnt."

"You think Maisie might turn me down?" Just saying it made my chest pinch. I could not imagine my life without her.

"If she's got an ounce of sense," he taunted, then sobered. "Only she can tell you that, but she hasn't run away yet." He pulled a droll face. "More to the point… have you told your parents?"

"No, but they must know it's serious. I take Maisie out every chance I get, all but declared my intentions to Mam that first afternoon, and it's not as though they're strangers. They *have* met twice."

"I know, but she probably did not expect it to last… none of your other dalliances did..."

I swallowed a wry grin. Joe made me sound as though I *was* the Don Juan of Nettleby. In fact, I had only ever attempted to ply my suit, twice. Both were friends from childhood and, naively, we imagined there might be more between us.

Neither courtship extended beyond one visit because, despite each young lady being quite lovely, we realised it was not meant to be. There was no spark, no heightening of the senses, nothing more than a vague affection formed over years of familiarity. Definitely not love.

"…and remember Maisie is not from the village. You will

need more than an 'I love her' to persuade your ma and pa, this is for life."

He was right. Convincing my parents would be a hurdle, but I had faith they knew me well enough to recognise that my feelings for Maisie were as sincere as they were profound.

Nettleby-under-Wold is a village unchanged since the first house was built… probably since the dawn of time. The same families have worked the land hereabouts for centuries.

There were periods when the population fluctuated then, somewhere along the way, it was as though a door had closed. From there on in, anyone not born in the village was viewed with suspicion — the Witch Finder General would be more welcome than an outsider.

In the last couple of decades, the village 'elders' had been forced to accept that the status quo was shifting.

Resentful at being expected to follow in their fathers' footsteps without question, several of the youngsters had broken free of the invisible fetters and ventured further afield, determined to carve out careers away from the land.

Engineering and teaching were popular choices. One or two had even gone into medicine — much to the disgust of their parents.

To be fair, most returned, thinking the village would benefit from their new-found expertise… or perhaps to show off.

Lizzie wanted to be a teacher, and her tomboyish tendencies had given way to quiet diligence. Personally, I thought it was a waste of time. Why work so hard at something she would be forced to abandon as soon as they married? For marry they will… of that I was convinced.

.   .   .

I dragged my mind back to my current predicament.

Joe was frowning at me. "Are you sickening for some-thing?" he quipped.

"Don't be daft. Just thinking."

"Ahhh, that explains the smell of burning."

"Cheeky bugger." I offered him a hand and hauled him upright. "Come on, them ditches won't clear the'selves."

Joe groaned and stretched his arms above his head. I heard his joints crack.

"You sound older'n me," I chuckled.

"Almost three years younger, and don't you forget it." He puffed out his chest, and thumped my shoulder.

After a brief and pointless wrestle — given neither of us won and it was too hot anyway — to prove our prowess, we were back at it.

As we laboured side by side, I acknowledged the confrontation brewing with my parents could not be put off any longer. I wasn't being true to myself or Maisie by delaying the inevitable.

Five

August 1908
Fred

Maisie and I were picnicking in the shade of a huge oak tree near the old churchyard at Holton-le-Moor.

A cycle ride, a tasty lunch, and a warm day had made me drowsy, but the huge knot in my stomach prevented me from dozing off.

It was Maisie's twenty-first birthday and I hoped it would be a double celebration.

Unbeknownst to her, I had visited her parents earlier in the week to ask her father whether he had any objections to me marrying his daughter. Mr Vickers, as anticipated, grilled me in the manner of an enemy soldier interrogating a captive, but I refused to be intimidated.

I felt quite proud of my fortitude until he peered at me over the rims of his spectacles and said, with a kind of wily glee, "You're sure you've given this proper consideration? You'll have your hands full with our Maisie. She's not your humble and demure type. She rushes in where angels fear to tread and dun't suffer fools gladly."

What a relief. Who wants a scared mouse for a wife? Not me.

"Then it is a good job I'm no fool," I had countered politely.

"Humph, time'll tell," was his crusty response.

I confess, the ordeal was something I never want to repeat. I even had to wipe my palm on my trouser leg before shaking hands with Mr Vickers.

In contrast, Mrs Vickers declared herself thrilled. She made me very welcome, plying me with copious cups of tea, and three too many slices of the best ginger cake I have ever eaten. It was even tastier than Mam's, a fact... valuing my health... I kept to myself.

Mrs Vickers insisted I take the rest of the slab when I left. "Go on," she had coaxed. "You look like you could use a bit o' flesh on them bones."

I added the cake to our picnic. Proof, of sorts, that I had done the gentlemanly thing. I planned the whole day in my head. Invite her out for a picnic, wait until we had eaten, ask for her hand.

I had the ring — it had been burning a hole in my pocket since the week after I persuaded her to accompany me to the café. It was my grandmother's, and she wanted me to have it for my bride, undeterred by my conviction that the chances of me marrying were doubtful to inconceivable. I could almost hear her shrewd chuckle, and her sly, 'I told you so'. Grandma would have approved of Maisie.

Apparently, the ring was considered a classic design. Whether that was true, I could not say, but I *could* say, the middle stone of the three on the thin gold band matched Maisie's eyes. A coincidence? Not even *I* believed that.

Now the moment had arrived, I was beset by the fear I ought to have asked Maisie if she wanted to marry me, *before* I spoke to her father. She might be one of those modern, independent women who refuse to be bound by the rules.

Unbidden, I recalled my sneaking suspicion, she was unconventional, however unintentionally. Joe's words bounced around my head… *You hardly know her, Fred.*

Scenes of the two of us flickered through my mind, and a strange calm descended. I might not know everything about her, but I *did* know she was the only woman for me, my soul mate, my guiding light, my mainstay. Without her I was adrift, and nothing was of any importance unless I shared it with her.

Not a sentimental chap, and reserved where emotions were concerned, I would only ever admit this to Maisie, and possibly Joe if he pressed me, but the strength of love I bore for my flower girl was immutable.

"Is everything all right, Fred?" Maisie's sleepy question penetrated my thoughts.

I twisted to look down at her, balanced on her elbows alongside me, studying me with those beautiful eyes, more grey than blue under the shadow of the tree.

"That all depends," I prevaricated.

She sat up straight and hugged her arms around her knees. Her expression, guarded.

"Fred?" There was no mistaking the faint tremor in her voice.

Now... I had to do it now. I retrieved the velvet box from my pocket. Awkwardly, given we were on a rug, I got up on one knee.

"My darling Maisie, we only met a handspan of time ago, but I feel as though I have always known you. On this your birthday, might I add to the celebration by asking whether you would do me the greatest honour of sharing a spot of tea with me for the rest of our lives?"

I opened the box to reveal the ring, praying she recognised the echo of my question from that first afternoon.

I watched her mouth fall open and heard her inhale sharply.

Maisie

I had heard the saying 'their jaw dropped' and presumed it was naught but a figure of speech to describe someone's shocked response. No… today, I learnt it is a physical reaction.

I knew something was bothering Fred, he had been fidgety all morning. I didn't think he was the kind of chap to upset his girl on her birthday, leaving me mystified as to the cause of his jitters.

Then, from being half-reclined, he shuffled onto one knee.
Opened a velvet covered box.
A ring winked in the dappled sunlight.
His words stole my breath and filled my heart.

That was when my jaw actually dropped.

Fred's dark gaze was wary. He ran a hand through his hair, his teeth worrying his bottom lip. It was adorable.

I started to smile, the joy welling up inside me bubbled over and I squealed, "Yes, yes, oh, Fred, a thousand times, yes." I flung myself into his arms with such enthusiasm we tumbled sideways onto the rug.

His kiss was the sweetest yet; tender and fierce, leisurely and fervent — a promise of forever.

A lifetime later, he raised his head. "Wait…" He fumbled with the box and removed the ring. Taking my left hand, he slid it down my third finger. It fitted perfectly. Three gemstones nestled in a simple gold band — a diamond either side of a stunning blue-grey stone. I stared at Fred.

"Fred, this is beautiful…" Even though I didn't add the 'but,' it hung between us. A ring so magnificent must have cost him his lifesavings.

Evidently, my thoughts were not as private as I wished because, with a knowing chuckle, he rubbed his thumb over the ring, then lifted my hand to kiss my knuckles.

"Don't fret, Maisie, this was my grandmother's. She told me aquamarine is known as the lucky stone. It was definitely lucky for her; she was married for fifty years. I'll wager we'll be luckier still, especially as it matches your eyes."

His dark gaze held mine. "That said, I would give my last penny to make you happy."

"I don't need your last penny. I don't need any money at all. I only need you." I scattered kisses across his cheek until our lips met.

The day went from marvellous to magical.

Six

December 1908 – Nettleby-under-Wold
Fred

The man staring back through the mirror was and wasn't me. Uncomfortable, I fidgeted, flexing my arms in the restrictive sleeves, and pulled at my collar. I was not used to wearing a suit and reckoned I looked ridiculous.

A knock at the door and Mam came in. Her face lit up and she clasped her hands against her chest.

"Son, you scrub up rather well." She brushed at the front of my jacket before twitching my tie.

"I feel stupid."

"Now, now. No Cuthbert is going to walk down the aisle in a pair of scruffy labourer's overalls. Have you no respect?" she tsked. "Think of Maisie. The lass wants her betrothed to outshine all the other village lads when she marries him."

I glanced at my reflection again. Reluctantly, I conceded

Mam was correct, I *did* cut a fine dash. I straightened my shoulders and practised a smile.

The man in the mirror looked terrified. I chuckled.

What was wrong with me? Today was the day that couldn't come soon enough, and now I was nervous.

Come on, Fred, I chided internally. *This is Maisie... not a stranger. She's the woman who makes your knees go weak and your heart hammer like it's about to burst clear out of your chest.*

I tugged at the collar again, only to have Mam slap my hands away.

"Leave it alone, Fred, or you'll turn up at church looking like a wet dish rag," she paused in her admonishment long enough to study me speculatively. "You love her?"

My cheeks reddened. "Yes."

Something in my tone satisfied whatever last-minute concern she harboured, and she patted my hand. "Good lad. I'll be in the parlour. Don't be long. Time's a wasting and you ought to be at the church afore Maisie."

She spoke to Dad as she descended the narrow stairs. His rumbled reply causing her to laugh.

My parents. I might complain they treated me like a child, but I loved them. They were pleased as Punch when I told them I wanted to marry Maisie. Mam asked why it had taken me so long.

After her initial reticence, she had come to like Maisie — to my everlasting relief. Same with Dad, who now considered her the daughter they never had.

Funnily enough, Maisie brought Dad and I closer. I have no idea how, but in the last sixth months, the relationship we shared when I was younger had been revived.

I rotated slowly around my empty and uncommonly tidy bedroom. Save what I stood up in, everything I owned was already at Maisie's... our... house. It would be odd not sleeping here.

Not having Dad thump on my door at five o'clock every morning on his way down to open the shop ready for the newspapers. Not hearing Mam chivvying me to get out from under her feet. Going from being looked after, to taking care of a house. To becoming responsible for two instead of one, and to paying my own bills.

I felt a smile hovering, banishing my introspection. My routine was about to alter dramatically and I could not wait to embrace the change.

Lacing up my shoes, polished so I could see my face in them, I looked in the mirror one last time, and followed Mam.

We were getting married at St Mary's in Wrawby, Maisie's local church, and every pew was full. The whole of Nettleby and half of Wrawby looked to have turned out, as well as Maisie's family and friends from Nottingham.

It was nerve-racking to be honest. I was certain I would trip over my feet as I walked down the aisle to where Joe was standing.

"Looking dapper there, Mr Cuthbert." He smirked.

"Leave it out, Joe."

"Not a chance."

We talked in undertones until I heard the strains of Maisie's favourite classical aria. The light touch of the organist made it seem like an ensemble of violinists were playing, rather than the sedate tones usually associated with the aged instrument.

I half-turned to see my bride framed in the arched stone doorway. My heart thudded and I lost my breath.

Her gaze never wavered from mine, as she floated down the aisle on her father's arm. Her exquisite gown, a vision of ivory silk and lace, whispered over the tiled floor.

She didn't look real.

I tried to imprint every detail in my head but, the minute she reached my side and smiled, I forgot everything except the fact that Maisie Vickers was about to become my wife.

Although brief, the ceremony was dignified. I think we sang a hymn and I remember signing the register, but the rest was a blur.

We were married.

December 1908 – St Mary's Church, Wrawby
Maisie

Snow blanketed the ground and dusted the trees. All sound was muffled. The weak sun hanging low in a pale sky had transformed the frosty ground into myriad shades of sparkling white.

On this winter's morning, Wrawby resembled a painting.

Dad and I walked up the church path, swept clear for the occasion.

"You must be nithered, lass," Dad chided, as we entered the porch.

I released the delicate fabric I had been holding clear of the ground, and shrugged the heavy cloak off my shoulders, folding it onto the stone bench to my right.

"This has kept me plenty warm," I reassured, "but I refuse to wear it during the service. Fret not, I am warm as toast."

He gave a long-suffering tut but forbore to comment further.

I squeezed his arm. "Trust me, Dad, I'm fine."

"You look beautiful." He kissed my cheek, and stretched

up to draw the veil over my face. He started to say something else, then stopped.

"What?" I implored.

"Are you sure this is what you want? To become the wife of a farmhand. To bury yourself in this tiny village in the middle of nowhere. You have such potential, Maisie, you could rule the world if you put your mind to it."

"Dad?" I was astonished. In general a reticent man, my father had never spoken to me on so personal a level or given any hint he felt I was blundering into marriage without due consideration. "I thought you liked Fred."

"I do, but…"

"Dad, look at me. Really look at me." I flipped back the veil to meet his gaze. "I love Fred, the mistake would be *not* to marry him. I'll still be working at the flower shop, and we'll be living in my house. I haven't given up any of my auton-omy, *he* is the one making compromises."

"That's another thing worries me, you going out to work after you're wed. It's not right."

Aware the congregation would know we had arrived, I maintained my composure. This was not the time for a discussion about the rights of women.

"Dad," I chided gently, using my best *I am your loving daughter* voice. "Mam worked until I came along, even then she did a bit of this and that. You know I cannot sit idle, and Mrs Barton is getting on. She finds it difficult to heft those buckets on and off the barrow. I'd like to think I might take over the business when she's ready to sell."

Dad gave me a hard stare, but whatever he saw quashed the rest of his concerns. "Well, you've always got a home with us if needs be," he said gruffly.

"I love you, Dad." I gave him a hug, and slid my hand around his crooked arm.

I heard the strains of the duet from the Pearl Fishers

opera. Fred might tease me about my love of classical arias, but even he acknowledged this piece was special. It was my favourite and the organist had declared himself happy to play it.

"I love you too, lass." Dad smiled, maybe a little tremulously. What with that and the haunting melody drifting out to us, I felt tears welling. I blinked, determined not to cry, this was my wedding day.

We stepped over the threshold into the cool interior, and I paused, entranced. Above the multitude of flickering candles, beams of sunlight through the stained glass windows had created wispy rainbows which formed and faded in the air, adding their own, almost ethereal, illumination. *A sign from God,* I mused whimsically.

I saw Fred waiting for me. Tall and handsome, his strapping physique encased in a dark suit. *Oh my...* my heart skipped a beat.

Our eyes met as I walked down the aisle, and I anchored myself in his fathomless gaze.

Almost before I realised the service had started, we were married.

Seven

August 1914 – Wrawby
Maisie

It was not quite dawn, but through our open window, I discerned a faint lessening of the darkness.

No, not yet. I was not ready. I would never be ready.

Snuggled against Fred, our limbs entangled, I wanted to stop time, to hold this moment for ever.

He stirred and shuffled until we faced each other. Levering himself up on one elbow, his fingers tiptoed from the curve of my thigh to the dip of my waist, and onward to tease and delight. I heard myself whimper, but whether in desire or distress, I couldn't tell.

Too soon he was dressed and at the door. His brand-new uniform hugged his burly frame, making me proud and sad.

Over the top, rather like a skeleton jacket, sat a thing called a pattern webbing — so Fred informed me — complete with numerous pouches, which were filled with all manner of equipment.

His regulation haversack, attached to the diagonal straps at the back of the webbing, was stuffed to bursting with as many changes of clothing as I could fit in. Great coats, rifles, and ammunition would be handed out when they arrived at the headquarters in Grimsby.

Initially, the brigade were to be stationed near the docks, as a first line of defence, but I knew, unless sense prevailed, they would end up in France.

He might get leave before that happened, he might not. I heard a whistle and saw Joe, with Thad Jenkins, striding along the quiet street. Against the backdrop of the pearlescent pink dawn light, they looked like ghosts, and I could not shake a sense of foreboding.

I pinned a bright smile on my face and kissed my husband. "You come home to me, Fred Cuthbert, do you hear," I instructed fiercely.

"It's only Grimsby," he teased.

"You know what I mean." I nudged his shoulder.

"Yes Ma'am." He bowed with a flourish and grazed his lips over the back of my hand. "I love you, Maisie." He swooped in for one last kiss, ignoring the ribald taunts from his friends.

"I love you too, Fred… and I'll see you soon."

"It'll all be over by Christmas, they say." He grinned and walked down the little path. The click of the latch on the gate sounded overly loud.

Greetings exchanged, the trio, in unison, turned to wave and then they were gone.

I leant against the doorjamb long after they had disappeared, as though by standing there, I still held onto him, that the act of going into the house and shutting the door would close a chapter of my life.

I wasn't ready.

Mittens, disgruntled at being disturbed at this ungodly hour, wove around my legs, mewling for food which, along with the chill of the morning, penetrated my senses. I gave myself a good shake.

"Can't stand here all day, Maisie Cuthbert," I chided. "The shop won't open itself."

Over the last few years, more by accident than design, I had begun to shoulder some of the responsibilities at the Cuthberts' shop.

What began as a helping hand while Fred's dad recovered from a nasty bout of pneumonia, had somehow transitioned into a more permanent role.

I *did* question whether this had been engineered, a way to stop me from fulfilling my dream of owning the flower stall. Uncharitable? Probably… but Fred's parents had never warmed to the idea and, I concede, I was less than gracious about being 'managed'.

Fred had assured me there was no underlying agenda and, funnily enough, once I got over my fit of pique, I genuinely enjoyed the work, especially running the post office. It fed some hitherto latent penchant for clerical organisation. Not that I apprised anyone else of this epiphany. Rather, I slowly tempered my frustration… no sense in letting them think they had won.

I refused to live over the shop though, despite the Cuthberts' oft repeated invitations. That it would save me an hour every day was not enough to convince me.

My home was my sanctuary, a haven away from all the hustle and bustle of the day, and a place for Fred and me…

no one else intruding on our private time. Yes, it meant getting up with the birds, but I was used to that anyway, working on the flower stall.

Thankfully, in this, Fred agreed wholeheartedly. He too relished the solitude of our home, of being able to close the door and shut out the rest of the world. Not to mention the extra space which came with having an entire house, as opposed to a couple of rooms.

As working arrangements went, it wasn't perfect, but it sufficed. When Fred got his departure date, his Mam had renewed her petition and begged me to move in with them for the duration.

"Makes sense, lass," she had wheedled.

"Perhaps to you, and thank you for your generosity, but I'd prefer to be where Fred's things are," I had tried to dissuade.

Mrs Cuthbert let it lie but revisited it sporadically in the hope, I would change my mind. To date, I had held fast.

While I tidied the bedroom, I realised, however compelling her argument, I could not leave this house. Everything had something of Fred in it, either by creation or use. The happiest times of my life had happened here, why would I leave?

He'll be home soon. I pushed all other worries out of my head and got on with my day.

Christmas came and went. The war showed no signs of ending. Almost immediately, Fred's unit was transferred from Grimsby to Belper, and on to Luton. He had been granted leave occasionally but, as I had predicted, that was no longer a possibility — he was bound for France.

He wrote as often as he was able, but it sounded like the

days were brim full of duties and tasks. His letters were hard to read because the censors scribbled out any sensitive information, even towns they had marched through on the way to their current destination — another mystery — somewhere in Flanders, I thought.

I didn't have much time to dwell on his absence, or wallow in self-pity. The shop kept me busy and, once we closed up for the day, I stayed back to balance the till and restock the shelves. I thanked the good Lord for Lizzie and Polly; we kept each other sane.

The conflict dragged on and, as those volunteering increased in number, the village seemed to shrivel. More than half the population remained but, without the young men, it was as though the beating heart had been yanked out.

Carefree evenings meeting Fred under the clock seemed so long ago.

Determined not to let our spirits languish, a couple of enterprising individuals had introduced a social night, and chivvied the villagers to attend, refusing to take no for an answer. Without fail, each Friday from six o'clock onwards, everyone descended on the village hall, where we played games, shared food, and had a singalong.

Before long, what began as a simple evening of light entertainment had become an elaborate affair, complete with competitions, quizzes, and displays. Soon, preparations monopolised everyone's free time, eclipsing the news trickling through from the front… to the organisers' relief.

Life in Nettleby ticked by. The year turned. Winter relinquished its grip, and the landscape took on every shade of green imaginable. Clumps of flowers appeared in sheltered corners, which, as the days warmed, flourished into a carpet of colour. The seasonal calendar of farm life lumbered on.

With so tranquil a backdrop, and save the lack of menfolk, it would have been easy to forget the discordant echoes of battle and death.

Until Lizzie received her letter.

July 1915 – Flanders
Fred

I stared at the blank sheet of paper and rolled the stubby pencil in my fingers, unable to credit I was penning this letter.

Soldiers are supposed to be cool, calm, and collected under fire and, to be fair, most of us were, but this made facing the enemy feel like a picnic in the park.

Cool, calm, and collected had deserted me when I sat down to write to my best friend's wife to inform her of his death. Not a task I ever expected to undertake.

Yes, she would receive an official notice, but this was Lizzie. While Thad, our commanding officer, would be as kind as possible, he had not the time to soften the blow — he had too many to write.

Finding the words to tell families their loved one

wouldn't be coming home was a thankless duty if ever there was one. Worse, he and Joe were second cousins — and, irrespective of the seven year age gap between them had always been close — he knew Lizzie almost as well as I did, and was devastated.

What sort of friend would I be if I did not add my condolences?

Blinking back a rush of unmanly tears, I did my best.

My dear Lizzie,

By now you will have heard from Thad. I do not wish to compound your grief, but I thought it might give you a modicum of comfort to know that Joe died a hero.

Our trenches were collapsing under the constant barrage of artillery, a situation exacerbated by the number of wounded requiring treatment, and heavy rainfall.

To my everlasting shame, it was my idea to create a diversion. All we needed was to get the Hun to fire in another direction, long enough to allow us to pull back to a safer series of trenches.

Thad and his fellow brass, who are all right as officers go, knew it was risky, and our options were growing thinner by the hour. It was a gamble, but we were trapped.

Ideas were pitched and, filtering out the unfeasible, we came up with an almost acceptable plan. Make it look like several sections were going over the top at an unexpected, illogical, and reckless angle, forcing the Germans to re-direct their artillery.

By the time they moved their guns and resumed firing, we had a reasonable chance of getting everyone else to comparative safety. The plan was flimsy at best, but it was all we had.

To my horror, Joe volunteered to lead the charge. I nearly shot him myself, but he would not be swayed.

Lizzie, Joe knew his was, essentially, a suicide mission. He and his mates would be extraordinarily lucky to escape unscathed, but if the few saved the many, he said he could live, he hoped, with that.

We watched them creep towards the end of the ruined trench system, until they disappeared out of our line of sight.

Ten brave men.

My heart was in my mouth and, for the first time in longer than I can remember, I prayed. With every fibre of my being, I prayed they would survive, that Joe would survive.

The firing stopped. There was an uncanny silence, followed by a series of explosions as the grenades detonated.

Then we heard them, screaming blue murder, as they went over the top, heading for the enemy line, guns rattling.

It worked. Lord preserve us, it worked. The Hun scrambled to swivel their weapons, desperate to repel what must have sounded like a horde of Tommys bearing down on them.

Eventually, they got themselves sorted and fired at their new target.

It gave us the window we needed to evacuate the weakened trenches. All the injured were removed to the field hospital and the line held, but none of the ten survived.

I bit my lip. Sometimes it was better not to go into detail. To tell Lizzie that a couple of men were only recognisable by a scar on a severed limb, or the pattern on a tattered sock was not what she needed to read. I chose tact.

Most, we couldn't find. They had vanished without a trace, as completely as though they had never been there. Even those we were able to identify would have died instantly and without pain.

We gained a morsel of satisfaction when we discovered the Germans had suffered grievously under the onslaught, as had their trench, which was duly abandoned.

That probably doesn't help you right now, but maybe in time it will be of some solace.

I am so sorry, Lizzie. I wish it could be different but, as I already said, your Joe was a hero. Without his courage and the bravery of the other nine, we'd all be dead or prisoners.

We all miss him. Joe was well-liked and respected among the lads, and I am honoured to have called him my best friend. My life was better for knowing him.

We are all thinking of you.

Fred.

I stretched; my back ached from hunching over. I had been writing for over half an hour filling two precious sheets with my scrawl, but it needed to be said.

Although the censors would probably strike out most of it, despite there being nothing to give away our position, at least, I had made the effort. Lizzie would appreciate it, and Joe would have done the same for Maisie had it been me who copped it.

The day was waning, the soft light of the summer evening finally giving way to dusk. Out of the blue I recalled the day Maisie and I met... officially. It had been an evening very much like this. *Maisie...*

Deliberately, I pushed the memory aside, rubbed my eyes, yawned, and stretched again.

"You writing to Maisie?" Charlie Townsend, a friend of Joe's from Wrawby, stuck his head around the wooden beam acting as a door jamb.

"No, Lizzie," I bit out harshly. The images flooded back in... *so much for that... thanks Charlie.*

Charlie's grin dropped. "I've written too. Had to, not right leaving it all to old Jenkins. Never seen a man look so blind-sided." He shook his head, pulled up the other stool and sank onto it, chewing his lip. "I hate this damned war," he muttered.

"Me too, but keep that to yourself, Charlie," I cautioned. "Morale is bad enough at the moment, and you don't want that lot crossing over to Blighty, do you?" I tipped my head towards no man's land. "We honour those ten by keeping this country and, therefore, England free." I held his weary gaze until he nodded. "Good lad." Conveniently forgetting he was only three years my junior.

I slotted the letter into the envelope, ready for the mail bag. "Come on, let's see whether there's any slop up for grabs."

Another day over and we were still alive.

Small mercies.

I wrote to Maisie, telling her what she would likely already know, and included the same details I'd given Lizzie. My wife and Polly, the other member of their trio, would get Lizzie through this.

I struggled to believe I would never see Joe again. I could not imagine how Lizzie would be feeling.

July became August. The war raged on. We held the line, but made very little gain, then again, neither did the enemy and, all the while, the death toll on both sides mounted as did the injury count.

It seemed utterly futile but — in defiance of the conditions, and the fear, and the odds, and the constant danger, and the rats, and the stench — our commitment to hold fast never wavered.

Care packages from home, along with the, thankfully, regular rotations out of the trenches to the encampment behind the lines, made life a tad more bearable… or at least, less oppressive.

I started a journal. A few of the men were doing it and, I confess, I was sceptical. *What was the point of recording what we saw every day, and who would want to read it? Not me.*

"It's not just for you, Corp'ral," Harry Alderton, another Nettleby lad, said one evening when I was grousing about it. "If 'owt happens to you, it's something to send back to yer missus."

"Don't tell me you write one too," I scorned, tempted to laugh, but something in his expression stalled my derision.

"Nothing is guaranteed, mate," he countered loftily. "You of all people should know that."

"Sorry, Harry. You're right," I conceded grudgingly. "It just seems an indulgence we can ill afford."

"I'll do whatever it takes to get me through each day." He grinned. "For me, it's a bit 'o time to gather me thoughts, like praying, only on paper not in your head." A faint flush stole up his cheeks at his admission, but he didn't retract his explanation.

Our conversation moved onto other things, but Harry's remark stayed with me. Since I had nothing else to do and nowhere else to go, what did I have to lose?

To my surprise, it was a cathartic exercise and, what began as a stilted list of daily chores, or the latest skirmish with the Hun, evolved into a picture of life in the trenches. Stories the chaps swapped about their lives; complaints about the hierarchy, the food, lack of supplies, the bloody Germans, the weather, even — *God help me* — feelings.

If I didn't make it, hopefully someone would send my diary to Maisie… it had become, in essence, a little piece of me.

Nine

August 1915 – Flanders
Fred

A t the end of August, I was on my first full day away
from the front for this rotation — and looking
forward to catching up on lost sleep — when a wild claim
spread through camp like a forest fire.

Joe had been seen.

Here.

I was quick to scotch the nonsense, but it refused to be
doused. This was ridiculous. Charlie told me he had got the
news from Jack Phillips, so I tracked him down and
demanded to know what the hell he was doing.

"It's true, Corporal, sir. I seen him with me own eyes. He's
pretty banged up, but he's alive. I wouldn't make up a thing
like that. I swear on the Holy Bible," the young private
insisted, all but bouncing in his excitement. "He's in with
Warrant Officer Jenkins."

I eyed him narrowly, and the image of that day, nearly two months earlier, reared up in my head. His assertion was impossible, but he sounded very certain. "Shan't believe it until I've seen him, Private, but thank you. And, by the way, no need to call me 'sir', Corporal will suffice." I dredged up a grin at his misuse of military titles, and he legged it.

The rumour ran all day. Something about being found under a horse and being treated for his wounds in a cushy billet — a farmhouse not five miles from camp. People had spotted Joe coming out of the Warrant Officer's tent, had seen him with the doc, with the quartermaster, having a bath, getting a shave.

Lo and behold, Phillips was right. I was sitting outside the tent, sipping the swill they called tea when a haggard figure, using a cane for support, appeared in front of me.

I stared, mouth agape in shock.

"Bloody hell, Joe... it really is you. Dammit man." I choked on my drink.

"Nice to see you too." Joe slapped me on the back, before sinking into the adjacent chair.

There was an odd silence while we contemplated each other and the enormity of what this meant. The ugly bruises Joe sported, weeks after the fact, were stark against his pallor, and the uniform they had given him, hung off his skinny frame. Not that the rest of us had an ounce of fat to spare, these days.

With studied casualness, I drawled, "Well, look at you, large as life and twice as natural. Thought the lads were pullin' me leg. There was me mourning your death and you were living it up in the lap o' luxury in a local farmhouse, in a proper bed 'n' all."

"Aye, after getting blown up and being buried in the mud under a dead horse, I fancied a little pampering," Joe parried with a tired wink.

I listened to his version of what happened, patently condensed, then said quietly, "I wrote to Lizzy. I told her what you did for us. Man, you're a hero."

"No, I'm not, Fred. I only did what anyone else would have done in the circumstances," he refuted.

I shook my head. "I know creating a diversion was my idea in the first place, but when push came to shove, I don't think I'd have the guts to carry out that particular plan."

"Yes, you would. If you thought it'd save your fellow soldiers, you'd do it in a heartbeat."

"Have you been able to contact Lizzy?" I changed the subject. No way in hell did I have Joe's courage.

"Not yet. Given I've been declared dead, there's no chance they would permit a letter to get through. I am being discharged with immediate effect." He tapped the cane lightly against his heavily bandaged right ankle. "Hopefully, I can tell her in person."

"Take a letter to Maisie, would you?"

"Of course!"

We talked well into the night, and four days later, Joe had gone.

I was happy for him but could have easily folded myself into his satchel among all the letters and messages for the folk in Nettleby, and hitched a ride home.

Instead, I hitched back to the trenches.

September 1915 - Nettleby-under-Wold
Maisie

The last couple of months had been awful. The loss of Joe Elliott had hit the village hard. He was the first of *our* lads to be killed in action.

While Lizzie was doing her best to keep a positive outlook, she was obviously struggling and, lately, had taken to sitting in the churchyard and talking about some great black dog. I'd never seen it, but she swore it wasn't fantasy.

Quite frankly, whatever got her through the day. I could not comprehend her grief. If it was me, I don't think I would have been able to get out of bed, still less face the constant stream of sympathetic sighs and well-meant commiserations.

Polly and I made sure she wasn't on her own too much, but Lizzie couldn't be persuaded to leave her house, and stay with either of us until life seemed less bleak.

"Joe is all around me there," she had said.

I understood. I would be the same.

It was a perfect September morning. High above, clouds — their undersides tinged with subtle rose gold — sailed across a sky whose blue appeared faintly veiled, and the sun was less brilliant. A sure herald of autumn, yet the warmth in the air promised a hot day ahead. Summer was not quite ready to relinquish its grasp.

I had woken with the dawn chorus, and decided to take advantage of the early hour to rearrange one of the shelves in the storage room at the back of the shop. I was hard at it when the bell tinkled.

"Be right there," I called, automatically patting my hair, praying the bun I had scraped it into had not unravelled. I was in luck.

I pushed aside the heavy curtain which acted as a door and came to a stupefied halt.

It was Joe.

I blinked and blinked again. My mouth worked but nothing came out. There was a rushing in my ears, then I felt a hand on my shoulder as someone guided me to the chair behind the counter.

"Maisie, Maisie, come on lass, it's only me." A rustle of paper followed by a brisk waft of air cut through the fog in my head.

I grabbed his hand and squeezed tightly, convinced I was having a nightmare.

"Hey, I might need that." He chuckled, peeling back my fingers.

"*Only you?* Joe Elliott, do you *want* to give me apoplexy? You're supposed to be dead."

"My humblest apologies, will a letter from Fred be adequate recompense for being alive and giving you a fright?"

"Joe, Lizzie...?" I shot to my feet, yet to be persuaded this was real. Thin, pale, and hollow-cheeked, his green eyes shadowed, Joe looked as though a strong breeze would flatten him. I reached out to touch him, muttering, "Just making sure."

His chuckle blossomed into a laugh. "I'm not an apparition. No, I haven't seen Lizzie. She's not at home, that's why I came here. Have you any idea where she might be at this time on a Saturday?"

I told him about the churchyard and the dog. "I think she's got a vivid imagination. I've never seen hide nor hair of such an animal around these parts. Mind, even if it's only in her head, it seems to comfort her, so who am I to question it?"

"Thank you, Maisie." A quick hug and he was gone. I leant

on the door jamb and watched him limp down the street, the tip of his walking stick crunching in the gravel.

Joe had survived. It still didn't seem possible. Fred's description of the charge had left me in no doubt as to the outcome. Apparently, miracles did happen.

I hoped my husband would be as fortunate.

Ten

June 1916 - Foncquevillers
Fred

Our regiment had been moved south to Foncquevillers — a sleepy nondescript hamlet, like all the other hamlets dotted along the front line between Arras and the river Somme, in readiness for a huge offensive.

It had become a never ending source of horror to me... aside from the obvious... that war compels its participants to travel to some of the world's most magnificent localities for the sole purpose of ruining that splendour with bombs, trenches, and bodies. All to save face. I still could not fathom the reasoning.

During the previous year, I had seen more of those places than most would get the chance to visit over several lifetimes, including an aborted voyage to Egypt. Me... Fred Cuthbert in *Egypt*. It's a good job there was a ship full of us, otherwise no one back home would believe me. I *did* write to Maisie, but suspected the censors had struck out the destination.

How on earth Egypt got involved, I had no clue. That was a total waste of time and resources, given the order was rescinded almost the minute we landed. We were on Egyptian soil for a measly three weeks. No exploring, no temples or pyramids... we never left the camp in Alexandria.

Since our arrival at Foncquevillers in May, following a stint at Vimy, we had spent most of each day lengthening and expanding the trench network, moving me to wonder how the once beautiful and unspoilt countryside now appeared to the reconnaissance planes circling above us.

Probably like an enormous web... if the spider had drunk one too many beers and forgotten the way home... with us, resembling an army of ants milling around in its tortuous trap.

Tactics were discussed and strategies prepared. Some of the information filtering down through the ranks made our hair stand on end, but we knew better than to question it.

The objective was Gommecourt, a village situated on a salient — a word which filled me with dread. An innocuous bulge in the landscape, these geographical features, while strategically advantageous always projected into enemy territory, leaving the troops defending them, vulnerable.

Around this time last year, Joe was injured at the Ypres salient. I tried not to look upon that coincidence as a portent of doom.

We were blissfully unaware this, seemingly, insignificant

piece of land was about to be indelibly etched into our consciousness. An element of what would become one of the most notable battles of any war in recorded history.

Our orders were to attack the north side of the salient, in part to cut it off from the Germans — in the main, as a diversion to protect the northern flank of the main offensive to be launched simultaneously a short distance to the south. Yet another hark back to last year... *diversions.* I had yet to see one end well for those doing the diverting and hoped this one would reach a better outcome.

No attempt had been made to keep our preparations under wraps. The enemy must be aware something major was afoot. Volleys of gunfire were exchanged but it was sporadic, as were the casualties... thankfully.

Then, the week preceding the battle, everything switched mode. Laying the groundwork for our assault, the British pelted the Germans with enough mortars to eradicate several countries let alone a front line.

Inexorably, zero hour drew closer.

The waiting was the worst. Nothing equips you for the moment of attack. Not the training, not the drills, not the encouragement from the officers and your comrades... nothing. Your mind refuses to settle, and gruesome scenarios writhe through your subconscious like tormented demons.

None of us was naive enough to suppose this would be a resounding success. The enemy — a formidable foe, and as committed to their cause as we were to ours — were not going to sit back and let us walk all over them. Loyalty, however misplaced — in our opinion anyway — is a powerful motivator. The likelihood of ending the day unscathed was marginal.

1ˢᵗ July - 07:00 hours - Gommecourt

The tension in the air was thicker than the morning mist. You could taste the barely suppressed fear.

Everyone prayed, if there was a bullet with your name on it, death would take you swiftly.

Our slumber was already stalked by the eerie wails of the wounded and dying. We did not need the dissonant melody to become a symphony of desolate shades, lingering among the poppies.

Attached to the 138ᵗʰ Brigade, our regiment was assigned to the reserve as a carrying party.

To an outsider this sounded like a safer position but, in fact — responsible for the resupply of whatever was needed in the way of weapons, ammunition, and the equipment necessary to hold any ground we gained — we were almost as vulnerable as the front line. Sometimes more so because of our constant movement up and down the grid of trenches.

We waited.

At 07:20, tendrils of smoke stole up from the left flank, expanding rapidly to obscure the attack front, and mask the first wave of soldiers who slipped over the top to hunker down at their designated positions in no man's land.

. . .

At 7:30, the signal went out and the battle commenced.

The German infantry had rushed to patch up the mass of barbed wire which, overnight, had fallen to a bombardment of Bangalore torpedoes. This delayed some troops, but others found gaps, capturing three trenches with minimal resistance.

I could never recall much about that day. I daresay at the time, every second, each step, every movement was brutally clear but, when I tried to summon up details, it was nothing more than dust and dirt, and a blur of uniforms.

All sounds merged into one deafening chorus of gunfire, exploding munitions, and ghastly screams. Perhaps it was my subconscious protecting me from the atrocities man was wreaking on his fellow man.

Despite early gains, the main assault by the companies we were supporting failed, and our unit was sent to hold a trench further up the line, where we ended up being pinned down for the rest of the day. We lost ten good men and one more wounded... an inconsequential number by comparison with the overall losses, but still hard to stomach.

It felt like the longest day of my life, yet it passed in the blink of an eye. Exhausted, we hoped for a reprieve but, as the gloaming transformed the landscape from devastated to picturesque, lulling tired minds, a new order came down.

"Relieve the 139th and be ready to go forward with the Leicesters to reach those believed to be holding out in the German's front line trenches."

Silence met the command, our expressions more eloquent than any words. This was no simple manoeuvre. The 139th were not around the corner, they were at Foncquevillers — the opposite end of our already overcrowded communications trenches.

Bloody, bugger, and sod.

My thoughts winged back to the previous July. It was almost a year to the day since Joe led the diversionary tactic, and little had changed. It was basically the same battle, just at a different point on the map.

Anger flooded me at the sheer senselessness. I wanted to lock the idiots who had started this in a small room without food or water until they called a halt and crawled back into their corners.

That the assassination of some tinpot royal had culminated in such widespread hostilities, beggared belief. There did not seem to be a way to end this without killing half of Europe... and for what?

In the countdown to midnight, a quiet discussion began amongst trusted comrades and, to a man, we reached the same conclusion. We should all — and by all, we meant both sides — simply drop our weapons and walk away.

Without soldiers there is no battle, without a battle there is no offensive, and without an offensive there is no war. Without troops, the combatants are reduced to a handful of leaders, whether they be kings, kaisers, or presidents. Let them fight each other to the death.

Yes, the subject was contentious, and we would never be stupid enough to repeat our observations to our superiors. We could all end up in front of a firing squad accused of being traitors for daring to *think* such things, never mind articulate them.

For those brief hours, as the darkness enveloped us, we weren't soldiers of the realm in a trench, we were a group of frightened and weary men, desperate to survive the night.

. . .

Just when we thought this nightmare could not possibly get any worse... it did. After belly-crawling through the under-growth to reach the other side of no man's land, we discovered the wire was uncut.

The enemy's defences at this section remained intact, meaning those trenches presumed to have been taken by our troops, had not.

Lie down and wait... those were our orders.

Lie down and wait... what the hell...?

We went from rescuers to sitting... or prostrated... ducks.

If oaths were bullets, the entire German army would have been annihilated.

Fatigue threatening, I thought about Maisie, and our reunion, deliberately recalling our last night together. Her eyes fiery with passion. Her lips branding me everywhere they touched. Her body writhing underneath mine.

The notion I might never see her again, or cause her sorrow, made me determined *not* to die in this dammed war.

The slightest movement resulted in a hail of gunfire. The injury toll mounted. I did not dare think about how many men had perished, for absolutely no gain. My anger became white hot fury, only nominally tempered when the retreat was called.

Under the protection of a Red Cross flag hoisted by one of the reserve divisions, we wormed our way back in the same manner as we had advanced, managing to collect some of the wounded. Too many had to be left where they fell, some of whom were taken prisoner.

Dispirited did not begin to describe the welter of emotions swamping us.

. . .

A brief but unilateral ceasefire was agreed, granting rescue parties a desperately needed respite to search for survivors, and retrieve bodies.

While a boon, it also served to highlight the inanity of this war. We could suspend the conflict long enough to extricate the wounded, only to resume hostilities the minute no man's land was clear.

Utterly ridiculous.

Our unit was tasked with the recovery, many of whom were from our own regiment. Not that this made any difference to our efforts but seeing my mates lying insensible and bleeding among the wildflowers was harder to bear, than when it was a stranger.

The sun was setting. Gunfire sputtered, shattering the peace. I was so tired, I couldn't tell from which side it originated, but it spurred on the last half a dozen of us. Charlie and I reached the ladder and hefted the unconscious soldier over the rungs into willing arms.

I heard the whine but didn't move fast enough.

A searing pain sliced through my shoulder. I heard myself bellow in agony, and the last thing I remembered was the ground coming up to meet me as I pitched forward, toppling into the trench headfirst.

Eleven

August 1916 – Wrawby
Maisie

I slid the knife along the seam of the envelope. Polly's letter arrived this morning, but I had saved it to read after the shop was closed for the day. Two pages fell out and floated to the floor.

I plucked them up before Mittens purloined them to shred, and unfolded one of the sheets. The words danced in front of my eyes, as I tried to work out why Polly was calling me darling. Shaking my head, I squinted, the better to focus.

My darling Maisie,

Polly has generously offered to write this letter and include it with hers to you.

Firstly, my love, please do not panic. I am alive if a trifle battered. I took a stray bullet to the right shoulder — the reason Polly is my scribe — two weeks ago and ended up in the field hospital.

I dropped into the nearest chair, as two things struck me.

One… Fred had been shot… *my Fred had been shot.* My world tilted sideways, and I clenched the thin paper, hearing it crinkle ominously. I had to force myself to slacken my grip, or the sheet would tear, and then where would I be?

Two… Polly had written on his behalf… *Polly.* I couldn't quite get my head around that and decided to come back to it later; Fred's letter was more important.

I took several steadying breaths and continued to read. Much of his explanation as to how he had sustained the injury had been blacked out by the censors, but I unravelled the gist. The rest was easier to follow.

Funnily enough, Polly was driving the ambulance. You could have knocked me down with a feather when I came to and saw her peering over the stretcher, but I was already flat on my back. It helped to see a familiar face.

Polly assured me it was just a graze, and that my arm was still attached. The doc was more concerned about my head given I landed on it when I fell into the trench. Took some ribbing for that, I can tell you.

Good news is, I'm recovering well. Bad news is, while I might warrant a spell in Blighty to recuperate, the long-winded procedure to organise leave means I would probably arrive just in time to be sent back. Much as I want to see you, it's less difficult to return to the front from here. I don't have the strength to kiss you goodbye again.

When the doc signs me off, I'll transfer back to camp for another week's rest before rejoining the lads.

There is so much I wish to say, Maisie, but I cannot find the words to do my thoughts justice. Best kept until I come home.

All my love,

Fred.

I read it three times, trying to work out whether he was hiding the truth from me, that his wounds were life-threatening.

Setting it aside, I picked up Polly's letter. She had written regularly since arriving in France, short missives about her work and the other medical personnel, avoiding any mention of casualties.

I had never pressed her for more details, if she wanted to share her experiences, she would. It *was* clear that she found her role rewarding if harrowing.

Until this moment I had no idea where she was based. I supposed such information was deemed confidential, but it was oddly comforting to know she was near the Lincolnshires, many of whom she would know by sight at least.

She reiterated what Fred had said, expanding a little on the nature of his injury. Her use of complex medical terminology made me smile. She sounded so serious and very professional… the antithesis of the fun-loving, carefree Polly who waved goodbye all those months ago.

My friend concluded with… *Please do not worry, Maisie. I promise you, Fred is recovering well. The doctor removed the bullet and, to date, there is no infection. He might be stiff in the shoulder for a while until it heals fully, but there ought not be any long-term damage.*

I am due on shift shortly, so I shall make sure this goes out with the next mail. Write soon. Reading about Nettleby is the highlight of my week.

Best wishes,
Polly.

Lost in thought, the letters clutched in my hand, I didn't move. The contents reassured and scared me. That Fred had been hurt, even slightly, tore at my heart. *Two weeks ago...* I glanced at Polly's letter, and counted backwards from the date, something about it teasing my subconscious... *why was it significant?*

With a jolt, it came to me. Fred was shot almost a year to the day since Joe had been declared missing, presumed dead, and I gained an insight as to how Lizzie must have felt when she received the notification.

At the time, her grief and sense of loss far exceeded what I was trying to process yet, suddenly, I understood why she had spent so many hours in the churchyard.

Out of the blue, I missed Pete. I could have done with his cheerful cheeping right about now. At the rustle of paper, Mittens, basking in a sun puddle on the rug, raised a bleary lid.

Uncoiling herself, she padded across and pushed her whiskery head against my calf. Absently, I picked her up and buried my face in her soft fur... ignoring her mewl of protest.

. . .

The loud rap of the brass knocker penetrated my reverie. Not in the mood for visitors, I ignored it. The rat-tat-tat persisted. Muttering balefully, I popped Mittens on the floor, and rose from the chair to answer the door.

On the step, Lizzie and Joe.

"Maisie, oh Maisie, we heard from Polly, she said she had written to you. Did you get her letter? We had to come."

I stared, unable to speak, wondering how Lizzie always seemed to know when she was needed. It was uncanny.

"You poor thing, I cannot imagine how scared you must be." Lizzie drew me into a warm hug, Joe following suit.

"I am fine, truly." Unaware the tremor in my voice belied my bright smile.

Lizzie studied me speculatively. "Cup of tea, that'll do the trick."

I saw her nod at Joe who headed to the kitchen. She chivvied me back along the hall to the parlour and sat me down, perching on the arm of the chair. "Polly did not give us the details but said her letter to you included one from Fred. Do you feel able to talk about what happened?"

Over her question, I heard the rattle of cups on the tray and the whistle of the kettle. Mundane, everyday sounds, and again reminded me of when we found out about Joe.

Polly had brewed tea that evening too. The solution to every problem.

As I sipped the steaming drink, the familiar aroma settled the whirlwind in my head, and I was able to tell them everything I knew — in truth, very little.

"Lizzie, your words are very kind, but my anxiety pales into insignificance compared with the grief you suffered last year. I know Fred is alive. You were not granted even that crumb of comfort." I said after answering their questions, as best I could.

"Hmmm… perhaps, but however difficult it was to come to terms with what I believed to be Joe's death, it was conclusive. Yes, I had lost him, but also I had lost my fears for him. He no longer had to confront an enemy determined to obliterate him and his fellow soldiers from the face of the earth. I did not have to worry about a minor injury festering, leaving him incapacitated and unable to escape, or even being taken prisoner."

Lizzie reached for Joe's hand, and they entwined their fingers. Their love was so strong it was almost tangible. "A quick death with no pain was less horrific than the alternative. So, no, I cannot imagine how scared you must be."

We chatted over another cup of tea, then they took their leave.

"You still coming to the singalong tonight?" Lizzie asked as they walked down the path.

"I'll be there." I mustered up a smile. An evening among friends was nearly as good a remedy for an aching heart as tea.

Twelve

August 1916 – Foncquevillers
Fred

To the backdrop of artillery fire, I trudged through the sinuous support lines in search of Thad Jenkins. Weaving my way around soldiers carrying supplies, I came upon a few of my division, sitting wherever they could find a comfortable position, cleaning their rifles, sharpened bayonets glinting in the sunshine.

I saw Harry glance up at the thud of my boots on the duckboards. He smirked, and I heard his low whoop.

All eyes swivelled in my direction.

"Well, as I live and breathe, if it isn't our one and only Corp'ral Fred Cuthbert." Harry effected a flourishing bow, reminiscent of medieval knights, as the others greeted me with embarrassing enthusiasm.

"Give over, I haven't been gone that long," I protested, unable to prevent a red stain flushing up my cheeks.

"We missed your ugly mug," Charlie quipped, and slapped my back... thankfully on my good side.

"No one to blame for our mistakes," Harry added...

...and the like was hurled at me.

Thad, presumably disturbed by the noise, poked his head out of a dugout about ten feet further along. He said something to whoever was within, then picked his way towards us.

"Warrant Officer Jenkins," I shook his outstretched hand. No coming to attention here.

"Glad to see you, Corp'ral." He didn't smile, as much as his weary features softened momentarily. "How's the shoulder?"

I flexed the offending limb, feeling and ignoring the painful spasm. "Nothing a decent beer wouldn't cure." I grinned.

Those who overheard sputtered with laughter.

It had become our catch cry. The assertion a pint of proper English ale could cure every malady from the sniffles to decapitation, had gone from a joke to restore flagging spirits to an unassailable conviction. It had even superseded tea... and nobody thought *that* was possible. Its mystical properties increasing in direct proportion to its scarcity.

"One day." This time Thad's face did break into a smile. "Welcome back, Fred."

An artillery round exploded a short distance from where we were standing, spraying us with mud. Instinctively, I ducked, but no one else even flinched.

"You'll soon get used to it again." Thad chuckled sympathetically, going on to explain our current duties.

Within half an hour, it was as though I had never been away.

It was a long hot summer. Here was I in France, a country I never expected to visit, surrounded by stunningly beautiful scenery — at least it was behind our lines, not so much in front — with no Maisie and no opportunity to explore. One more black mark against this bloody conflict.

Instead, we were maintaining and holding the trenches between Foncquevillers and Berles-au-Bois. Our days consisted of tedious routine interspersed with short bursts of frenzied activity, and boredom became a greater foe than the enemy.

Wise to this, when we rotated out, our superiors endeavoured to counteract the monotony. Amidst marching, drill, and associated military chores, competitions intended to challenge us mentally and physically were organised, leaving little time to laze about. Boxing, athletics, and football were easy favourites.

Relatively safe from ambush or sniper fire, one could almost forget we were in the middle of a war…

…almost.

Those of us who had scrabbled to recover our casualties when the ceasefire was called following that horrendous day in July… scant weeks yet several lifetimes ago… had been recommended and approved for a Military Medal for bravery under fire.

We supposed we ought to be honoured but, given how many of our comrades had succumbed to their wounds, it seemed an odd and rather tactless accolade. We didn't do it in hope of glory, we did it to save our friends.

Still, I could understand the regiment's pride that their number included several recipients.

The days blended into one, and before we knew it, summer gave way to autumn. As the air lost its heat, the palate of the landscape was revived. Tired greens made way for gaudy hues — bronze, gold, red, and purple. An artist's delight, and a soldier's misery.

Temperatures plummeted. Incessant rain replaced cloudless skies, frost nipped exposed skin, and dry trenches became rivers or quagmires. It didn't matter what we did, the cold seeped into our bones, trench foot was rife, and, despite every precaution, no one escaped the raft of ailments sweeping through the troops.

Later... much, *much* later... we discovered that this winter was the coldest in living memory. I needed no convincing and would not have been in the slightest surprised had polar bears or penguins been spotted patrolling no man's land.

The wretched weather played havoc with my old wound. The surgeon had stitched me up well, but the ache never really diminished. Even knowing it was all in my head, sometimes I swore the bullet was grinding against the bone, and surmised the reduced sensation in my hand was not solely related to the cold.

It compromised my ability to hold a rifle and, although I had made a concerted effort to use my left arm, my accuracy was woeful. Not that I was prepared to admit this to anyone, and continued to practice but, by mid-November, I struggled to move my right arm at all. I could not swing a shovel, let alone dig a latrine. My dogged attempts to disguise the crippling pain, were in vain.

November 1916 – Foncquevillers
Fred

Thad Jenkins summoned me to his dugout.

"Corporal Cuthbert, while I applaud your dedication to duty and diligence, you are now risking more than your own life. Much as I would like to keep you here, for the morale of the unit if nothing else, I cannot have an incapacitated soldier under my command."

I tried to explain, but he was adamant.

"There is no argument you can make to change my decision; all it requires is approval by the medical board. I'm sorry, but if they agree with my recommendation, I have no alternative but to discharge you from service."

I gaped at him.

His grave demeanour relaxed, and he became the friend I knew from home, not my ranking officer.

"Fred, you must see you cannot go on like this. You think I'm not aware of the pain you're in? To say nothing of the fact, you're an appalling shot when you use your left arm. Won't need the Germans to finish us off, we'll end up killed by friendly fire." His chuckle took the sting out his reproach.

I realised any appeal was futile and, in all honesty was unsure why I thought one necessary, but allegiance to my division, my mates, died hard. Much as I wanted to go home, I felt like I was abandoning them.

We talked for a little longer, then Thad wished me all the best, and a safe journey home.

The lads, neither blind nor addled, had guessed the reason for the impromptu interview and, in no uncertain terms, told me not to be an idiot.

"If you can hoist your rifle with your right hand, aim, and hit that tin can, WO would let you stay in a heartbeat," Harry contested.

I looked at the faces of those around me, their pleasure, one of their number was about to escape this hell was not feigned. They were genuinely glad.

"If you can write fast, I'll hang around and take your letters."

"See… silver linings." Charlie grinned.

Thirteen

Fred

Dispatched to the encampment, I was examined by the same field surgeon who had fixed me up.

"Sorry Corp'ral," he said solemnly, "I can't let you go back up the line. I'll have to sign you off as unfit for duty."

My desire to hug the man for this deliverance, warred with my innate sense of loyalty to my regiment, neither did I want anyone to deem me a coward.

He read my mind. "Corporal Cuthbert, this is not a dishonourable discharge. You took a bullet, which although a through and through, chipped the bone and tore the internal structure of your shoulder… muscles, tendons, and nerves.

"We repaired what we could, but there was always a risk the damage was too great, especially given the strain on your shoulder caused by repetitive actions like firing a rifle or digging trenches. I suspect the damage has been exacerbated by the deplorable weather of late, not to mention the atrocious conditions.

"If I ignore the warning signs and permit you to return to the front, not only is it a dereliction of *my* duty but also, if I do so, you are likely to lose the arm." He studied me over the rims of his owlish spectacles.

"I didn't think it was that bad." I shuffled awkwardly, downplaying the pain, which, from a vague throb, had intensified to what felt like red-hot pokers being jabbed into the joint.

The surgeon raised a brow at this massive understatement. "You cannot fight my prognosis, Corporal. Be thankful you are going home almost intact. Of course, my recommendation must be endorsed by the board and the colonel, but, I guarantee both will be a formality in your case."

"I *am* thankful, it's just…" I let that trail off. I did not need to articulate my dilemma.

To an outsider, I looked uninjured. My legs still worked, my brain was sharp, my eyes were clear. I wasn't sure what was worse, facing the Hun, or facing the accusatory whispers of those back home who assumed you had shirked your moral obligations to King and Country.

"I imagine everyone in your neighbourhood knows you are over here," the medic contended. "Don't worry about the possibility of a maybe." He tapped his chin, thoughtfully. "Also, if recent briefings are credible, and I have no reason to doubt them, you're entitled to the Services Rendered Badge. Marks you as honourably released from the army owing to wounds received during the conflict."

He was right. With everything else going on, I had forgotten, but his words reminded me of Maisie's last letter. She mentioned Joe had received one.

The little silver medal — an initiative of King George and first issued two months ago — was introduced to affirm those wearing it were no longer able to serve by reason of illness, injury, or disability. The relief resurfaced, and I allowed myself a grin.

I was going home.

The afternoon was taken up with the medical board, who put me through a gamut of tests, none of which shed me in a physically fit light… to my disgust. As predicated, they agreed with Thad and the surgeon.

I stopped arguing.

The next couple of days vanished under a pile of paperwork. Forms and more forms, and enough instructions to give me a blinding headache. Grumpy didn't begin to describe my mood by the end of it.

All I wanted to do was find my bunk, and write to Maisie to let her know, even though I had no idea when I might actually leave. The process of being signed off from this war was far more convoluted than signing up.

On top of all the other documents, I was told to keep on my person until officially released, I had letters from the field surgeon and the medical board, respectively. These were to be presented to my own doctor because, in their expert opinions, I would require ongoing rehabilitation.

By the time they dismissed me, I could scarcely keep my eyes open, and it was all I could do to scribble a letter to Maisie, before falling asleep without bothering to eat.

A first.

As soon as I had a moment to spare, I sought out Polly, tracking her down to a field at the edge of the camp where they parked the few vehicles at the hospital's disposal. I swallowed a grin when I saw her dressed in scruffy overalls, peering into the engine of an ambulance... the antithesis of the Polly I was used to seeing... spick and span, with never a hair out of place.

I hoped she wasn't overdoing things. While unfailingly positive, she looked as exhausted as the lads in the trenches.

Her, "I'm fine, Fred," sounded like she was convincing herself not reassuring me. She rubbed oily hands on an old rag and kicked a wheel. "I spend more time fixing these bloody ambulances than driving them."

"Please take care, Polly," I implored. "It's a dangerous business..."

I didn't get to finish my sentence.

"Don't say it, Fred," she muttered. "It's bad luck. Give my love to Maisie and Lizzy. Safe travels." She fished about in a pocket, withdrawing two letters, which she asked me to add them to my growing pile. "I've been carrying them around," she said, in oblique apology for their crumpled appearance.

I pretended not to see the suspicion of tears on her grubby cheeks. A quick hug accompanied her goodbye, and she hurried away.

"Look after her," I murmured to the heavens.

December 1916 - Nettleby-under-Wold
Maisie

Winter came so fast on the heels of summer we hardly had chance to enjoy the colourful blaze of autumn. Unseasonably early snow turned the landscape from heat-worn green to dazzling white, almost overnight.

Suddenly, the chill air was redolent with aromatic smoke as numerous bonfires consumed the fallen leaves. Icicles festooned gutters and lampposts, their jagged iridescence creating a multitude of shimmering rainbows. Hoarfrost transformed distorted trees into elegant sculptures.

The ground, hard as iron, became treacherous underfoot to the detriment of the unwary. Children, blissfully oblivious to the disruption the weather was causing around the country, cavorted in the powdery snow and skated along frozen roads with unabashed glee.

All manner of deliveries were delayed, including the mail, and it was early December before Fred's letter reached me.

I almost missed it. There was a mountain of post to sort through and, somehow the slender envelope ended up in someone else's bundle. It would have circled back to me eventually, but I spotted Fred's handwriting at the last minute, and retrieved it.

The shop was busy. Word had gone around that a train, bearing supplies, had made it through, prompting a never-ending queue of people intent on emptying the shelves as fast as we filled them. I told Fred's mam, I would pop upstairs later and we could read the letter together.

She sent me a harried smile, her attention on Mrs Hubbard who had a list as long as her arm, and who insisted on reading out each item individually rather than handing it over, which would have been much quicker.

I rolled my eyes in sympathy, and carried on.

It was gone seven before we closed up shop, and I inhaled the stew, Ma Cuthbert had shoved in front of me.

"That was delicious," I sighed, replete.

"Aye, you could do with a bit more flesh on your bones," she chided, tolerantly.

"I eat."

"Not enough."

"Leave the lass alone." Mr Cuthbert chuckled at our banter. "She looks fine as she is."

"Thank you, kind sir," I beamed at my father-in-law, who twinkled back at me.

It was an ongoing exchange. Fred's mother had a heart of gold, and never stopped worrying that I didn't eat enough, regardless of how many times I assured her that I liked my food too much to go hungry. A concern, I chafed at when first expressed — around the time Fred left — had become a source of shared amusement.

"Never mind my eating habits. Do you want to hear what Fred has to say?"

His parents nodded, and I opened the letter, scanning it quickly. It was shorter than his usual correspondence, and I felt a shiver slink down my spine, nothing to do with the draft creeping around the edge of the door.

My darling Maisie,

I blushed when I read the endearment and ignored the sidelong glances of my two listeners.

I checked the next line before continuing just in case I ought to skirt over it.

I am coming home.

I made a strangled sound at the bald announcement. "He's coming home."

"What? When? Why?" The pair quizzed in unison.

"I have no idea, let me read on."

The injury to my shoulder has rendered me unable to perform my military duties, which resulted in me being discharged. My departure date has yet to be confirmed but should be within a week or so.

I glanced at the top of the letter... 13th November... it had taken nigh on three weeks to reach me. There was every chance he was on his way. Goodness, he might be nearly home. I dampened down my excitement, not daring to believe.

I will send you an update as soon as I receive my orders. I just wanted you to know.

I cannot wait to see you. Please give my love to Ma and Pa.

All my love,

Fred.

P.S. Told you it'd be over by Christmas... well for me anyway.

That was it. More a note than a letter, but it was enough.

He had kept his promise.

Fourteen

December 1916 – Brigg Station, Lincolnshire
Maisie

I waited under the clock.

The mass of humanity thinned as each soldier was met, hugged, and wept over. Joyful cries rang out over the frigid air as hope was revived.

I scanned the platform, no familiar figure walking my way. Where was Fred? Was he really coming home, or had he been killed, and I was here to take possession of a coffin? *Maisie you are being irrational*, I berated internally, dousing the flash of panic. *Fred has written for heaven's sake.*

In quick succession, two more letters followed his brief note, the final one outlining his travel details, even confirming he was in possession of the train tickets. Each one penned by my husband, not some formal missive from a faceless official.

Irrespective of this, I fought to quell a mounting fear, which heightened as the crowds diminished.

In a matter of minutes, I was the only one left, but the train hadn't moved. Compelled to stay until there was no hope, I blinked back despondent tears. Our long-desired reunion wasn't destined to be today.

Movement at the end of the platform caught my eye. A tall man and Mr Watson, the guard, were helping a passenger off the train. Frowning, I glanced around expecting to see another family waiting but, save those three, I was alone.

Ready to offer assistance but without making it obvious, the pair walked alongside their charge whose gait was awkward as though each stride caused him discomfort. He looked vaguely familiar but my whole attention was fixed on his companion…

…who, right at that moment, lifted his head.

My breath froze in my lungs.

My heart pounded, stopped, then began to race.

"Well, there's a sight for sore eyes. If it isn't my flower girl." The deep rumble of his voice floated to me on the breeze.

"Fred," it was no more than a whisper, but he heard.

Mr Watson glanced up, and saw me. He said something to Fred, but I didn't catch it. They shook hands, and Fred hung back while the duo continued their slow way along the frost-dusted, grey concrete.

As they passed me, I recognised Harry, one of Fred's friends and, abstractedly, reached out to squeeze his hand. He grinned a weary greeting and was gone.

The sound of the whistle jolted me from my daze,

galvanising me, and I flew along the platform as the train began its ponderous haul out of the station, steam enveloping everything in its wake.

Through the mist, I saw Fred drop his haversack and open his arms.

Then I was wrapped in his embrace to be kissed with intoxicating sweetness, as endearments tumbled off his lips. I clung to him, yet to be convinced I wasn't dreaming.

He looked gaunt and haggard and had lost a lot of weight, but he was here. That was all I cared about.

Fingers entwined, we strolled home through the encroaching twilight, our breath coming in little white puffs as we talked. Well, I talked, Fred interjected an odd comment here and there, but seemed content just to listen.

When we reached the door, he stopped.

I turned to study him in the gloom, his face was etched with fatigue.

"Is something amiss?"

"I am savouring this moment," Fred murmured.

I waited, sensing there was more to come.

"To cross the threshold into my home with you at my side was something I took for granted. No more. It is a blessing. A privilege afforded to fewer and fewer men."

I unlocked the door, pushed it open and stood to one side.

"Then you should go in first."

He took my hand, and drew me close for another heady kiss. "No, we go in together."

December 1916 – England
Fred

The train journey up country was interminable. The last leg in a protracted process. I had travelled from Foncquevillers to Abbeville where, after being subjected to further medical checks, I wrote to Maisie. Then, on to Dieppe, suffering a choppy crossing to Portsmouth.

From there I *had* hoped to board the first train to London and on to Brigg… no such luck. Bound by military protocols, I was escorted to the dispersal centre to be examined... *again*. I sympathised with Pavlov's dogs.

After two days of what to my farmer's brain seemed like a repeat of the procedure at Foncquevillers, they stamped my papers, and told me to keep them safe as proof of discharge. I was handed three train tickets, the first taking me to London Victoria the next morning.

Three days hence, I would depart Kings Cross for Newark, from where I would transfer to the Grimsby branch line. I was frustrated about the intervening days in London but, according to the officials, it was unavoidable.

I was informed about a hostel not far from Kings Cross, set up for returning military personal. Apparently, it had all the amenities, which sounded wonderful, but I didn't need a holiday, I needed to get home.

Generously, the administrator — patience personified, undoubtedly, a requisite trait for such a tedious role — agreed to add a letter to the mail bag, and I dashed off a few lines to Maisie telling her the date I was due to arrive home… bar unforeseen delays. Then he organised transport to the station.

I was astounded at the reasonably large crowd of men already huddled in the waiting room. Evidently, a regular occurrence because a trestle table had been set up and several charitable souls were doling out hot soup, fresh bread rolls and steaming cups of tea… as much tea as we could drink.

After what I had been used to, it was ambrosia. We hadn't starved, but the mess was limited in what they could offer, and it had reached the point where we joked that the duck-boards in the trenches would taste better than what they served.

Throughout the hours of darkness, demob happy, we talked, sharing stories of our experiences. Shortly after dawn, our desultory chatter was interrupted by the laboured chug of the train.

We boarded only to sit for hours… everything seemed bound by the premise of hurry up and wait.

Not one of us complained.

We were on home soil.

Three Days Later
Fred

Kings Cross was bustling, even at this early hour. Neat queues of serge-clad soldiers prepared to board. Different accents and the occasional kilt attested to the length of their onward journey, and the pervading mood was cheerful, even in the wintry chill of the sunrise.

A hand clapped my shoulder and I spun around, my jaw dropping when I saw it was Harry Alderton. He looked terrible. A bandage peeked out under his cap, and his face was marred by several lacerations.

"What the dickens?"

He tapped his ear.

I repeated my question, slowly and loudly.

"Got blown up," Harry's voice lacked its usual chirpiness, and his words were distorted.

"Told you smoking near the ammo dump was bad for your health." I remembered to speak with deliberation.

It transpired, he was wounded the day I left the front line and, after a stint in the field hospital was being sent home for extended leave. Although his injuries were relatively superficial, his hearing had been badly affected and he was no use to anyone, deaf.

It was up to his doctors to determine whether he would go back.

We found two seats together, but Harry dozed off almost before the train left the station. I was content to admire the English countryside through the soot-smeared window. Acres of glistening snow in myriad shades of white gliding by, interrupted by the occasional settlement.

Inevitably, my thoughts winged to Maisie.

Two years… more… since we had last seen each other. It was an age. I knew of soldiers whose wives or sweethearts had not been able to endure the separation, and praised the good lord, my flower girl was as honest as the day is long. I wagered, I knew Maisie well enough that had something been awry, emotionally, I would have discerned it in her letters.

Today, before nightfall, I would get to kiss her and hold her in my arms. To reaffirm the vows we made years ago, words I had begun to question, I would ever have the chance to say again.

It didn't seem real.

The jolt of the train, the smell of pipe smoke, and the laughter of my travelling companions told me this was no dream.

I counted the stations from Newark. Harry was wide awake now, but it was clear, concentration of any kind tired him.

We confined ourselves to pointing out the increasingly familiar landmarks as we passed.

The afternoon was waning, dusk fell early at this time of year, the sun already dipping towards the distant horizon. The sky — reminiscent of Maisie's flowers — morphing from periwinkle blue to lavender and violet, tinged with rose and carnation. I grinned at my nonsense, while secretly impressed I had recalled the names of the different blooms.

A shrill hoot drowned out the chatter in the carriage and the train decelerated. I leant against the window and peered through the smoke. The platform was heaving; a throng of people milled about.

I was gripped by nerves. *Would I recognise my wife? Would she recognise me? What if she wasn't there…* my thoughts spiralled out as the doors opened.

Cold Lincolnshire air drifted in and I heard the station master shout, "Brigg, Brigg Station."

"Harry," I nudged him and inclined my head towards the door. Once he was upright, I tucked my arm under his elbow. The guard, coming along the train to check for stragglers, helped us onto the platform.

"Thank you, Mr Watson." I dipped my head, pleased I remembered his name. Stretching, I breathed deeply, filling my lungs with the scent of home.

His wrinkled face creased into a smiled greeting. "Glad to see you back in one piece… almost. Come on, Harry," he encouraged. "Nearly home. Looks like the pair of you are due a long rest."

"You won't hear any argument from me." I grinned.

I looked up.
There she was.
Under the clock.

I could see her pink hat, reminding me of the day we met… or, at least, the first time I dared strike up a conversation. My lips twitched. My wife knew how to stand out from the crowd… as though that was in any way necessary.

"Well, there's a sight for sore eyes. If it isn't my flower girl."

My heart drummed and it was all I could do not to gallop along the icy concrete. Only Harry's pained stride held me back.

Spotting Maisie, Mr Watson chuckled. "Go on, lad, what are you waiting for? I'll take care of Harry. The lass'll be about bursting out of her skin to see you."

"Thank you," I replied, and shook his hand absently, barely aware the two had continued along the platform.

I dropped my kit-bag and opened my arms.

She flung herself into my embrace. I kissed her with an ardour that would take weeks to slake, murmuring my love for her again and again.

I was home.

Fifteen

April 1917 – Nettleby-under-Wold
Maisie

Survivor's guilt is a terrible burden.

In the aftermath of Fred's return, the nightmares were the worst. Every night for weeks, he thrashed and tossed, only rousing under my careful shaking, his voice reduced to a hoarse rasp, his eyes glazed.

I worried about what the neighbours might think, only to discover Fred was not the only one. Joe still fought a constant battle to get a decent sleep, the torment stalking his rest — and the same applied to the handful of others who had been discharged for one reason or another.

Taking his visible injury into account and, while not naive enough to presume Fred would escape the chaos unscathed, nothing could have prepared me for the severity of his anguish.

It continued for a couple of months, until Lizzie and I

decided enough was enough and, one sunny afternoon in early spring, we took them to the top of the wold for a picnic.

As far as the eye could see it was peaceful. Here and there, figures moved across the landscape — small from our vantage point — tilling the fields, feeding the animals, tending to crops. The snow had melted to reveal a patchwork quilt in verdant greens, and the trees were laden with buds.

Clumps of daffodils, crocuses, and lungwort danced in the breeze, their fragile blooms — a welcome sight after the endless white of the harsh winter.

A few bicycles whizzed along the roads and, in the distance, the drawn out *tooooot* of the train as it pulled away from the station, a trail of smoke in its wake.

We laid out the food, poured the drinks, and gossiped about nothing of any consequence while we ate every last morsel.

I looked at Lizzie and, at her discreet nod, launched in.

"This can't go on, lads. You, Fred, look worse now than when you got off the train." I made a concerted effort *not* to sound like a school ma'am. "You need to talk to us about what happened, what you witnessed. Talk about it over and over and over again, until you are fed up talking about it but can do so without it haunting you as acutely."

"It's not fit for ladies' ears," Fred protested, running a hand though his unruly hair.

"What, you mean the bodies, and the blood, and the gore?" Lizzie interjected wryly.

Both men gaped at her.

"B-but… h-how?" they chorused in unison.

"You think your nightmares are silent?" She pinned them with a shrewd grey gaze.

I took Fred's hand, and interlaced our fingers. "I'll wager I can give a blow-by-blow rendition of particular battles, down to what time you went over the top, who was injured, who was killed, how many horses were hurt, how much ammunition was used. Need I go on?"

I smiled, perhaps a little sadly. "I understand you wish to protect us from the horror, but *you* need to understand, we are experiencing it every night, through you."

Fred and Joe shared a glance, looked at us, then back at each other.

Fred shrugged, feigning nonchalance. "I s'pose it couldn't hurt. If, you're sure."

"I would rather hear about the trauma you suffered, however gruesome, than be shut out," I replied. "You have no idea how helpless we feel."

Lizzie nodded her agreement. "It's not healthy. You are reliving it to the point where it is consuming your lives."

"You need to work out how you can be whole again, without shouldering blame," I added my entreaty. "War is a travesty and continues to rip people apart even after they have returned home, but just take a moment to look, really look at this."

I spread my arm out, encompassing the endless view. "This is what you did… you saved *this*. Without you and those who sacrificed their lives, this would be gone."

"No, it wouldn't," Fred argued. "You can't alter the land-scape. It's ancient, immutable."

Lizzie and I raised our brows.

"Oh really?" Lizzie countered. "What about the trenches and the foxholes? What about no man's land,

and the craters filled with black mud, and the graveyards?"

"How do you know about that?" Joe tried to deflect.

"Did you hear what Lizzie said about the nightmares? Not to mention the newspapers are full of the war." I paused and swung my gaze between them. "We might live in a sleepy village, but that does not mean we are oblivious or immune to what's happening."

I took a breath. There was something else. Something I had intended to tell Fred later, in the privacy of our home but it dawned on me... *now* was the perfect time. My news was providential, the distraction Fred needed, a way to start the healing process.

I had buried my sadness that I did not seem able to give Fred a child so deeply, it was naught but a faint prickle in my subconscious. Lizzie was over seven months gone, and when she told me she was expecting, while ecstatic for her and Joe, it had catapulted our own lack of children into sharp focus. Eight years since we wed... I had given up hope.

"Sometimes war accords us unexpected gifts." Unaccountably shy, I felt my cheeks pinken.

The other three stared at me, incredulous.

"Do please elaborate," Fred scoffed sarcastically.

"I am not saying war itself is a gift, but maybe reunions can produce surprises," I said, less than coherently.

Their matching bafflement had me stifling a wild giggle.

Lizzie laid the back of her hand against my forehead. "No, she's not running a fever," she teased.

Joe spluttered with laughter.

"Maisie?" Fred pressed, ignoring them.

"The restoration of our lives is not the only thing your return has blessed us with."

His brows knitted. "I think I'm going to need a little more."

I heard Lizzie give a low whoop, but didn't react.

"I'm nearly four months pregnant." I held his velvety brown gaze.

There was absolute silence.

It lengthened until I didn't know whether to scream or slap him.

"Say that again," Fred croaked, his stunned expression comical.

With a gentle smile, I repeated my declaration.

He blinked and swallowed. "We're going to have a baby?"

I nodded, my reply caught in my throat at the love shining from his eyes.

"How did I miss that?"

"You were otherwise occupied." I dimpled, the pink flaring to bright red.

He grasped my hand, hauled me to him and, uncaring that our friends were right there, kissed me into insensibility.

"I love you, my flower girl."

"The sentiment, Fred Cuthbert, is entirely mutual," I replied.

The day became one of celebration, the trauma of war relegated to the fringes for a little longer.

Epilogue

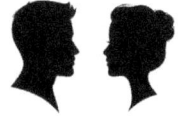

September 1939 – Nettleby-under-Wold
Maisie

Three couples huddled around the wireless, listening to Mr Chamberlain's dreaded announcement.

It was happening again.

The six of us looked at each other in horrified disbelief. Was not the last war to end all wars enough? Had the countless deaths and casualties, meant nothing? Was their sacrifice wasted?

Worse, this time our children would be drawn into the madness.

Unbidden, I recalled Fred's journal. We had read it together in the days following that memorable picnic, curled up on the sofa in front of a cosy fire.

The tranquillity of our home and the tragedy of conflict

were in stark contrast but, curiously, that very disparity helped me comprehend the enormity of what he had endured.

I wanted to scream at the lunacy that had spawned this momentous proclamation. The weapons at the world's disposal were significantly more devastating than those wielded in 1914, their destructive power limitless.

The future darkened.

Fred reached for my hand, clasped it tightly and kissed my knuckles.

November 1939 – Brigg Station
Fred

The train drew to a halt and disgorged its passengers. Mayhem ensued as people bustled about like a flock of sheep without a sheepdog. A semblance of order emerged from the confusion, and those boarding the train were no longer hindered by the hordes disembarking.

The guard blew his whistle and, in a flurry of hugs and well-wishes for a safe journey, the platform emptied, save four people.

Joe, his arm around a sobbing Lizzie, waved, mouthed a goodbye, and led her through the elegant brick concourse to their car.

Now there were only two.

Under the clock, Maisie and I remained motionless, until the train disappeared from sight. Hope, our eldest daughter, and Thomas, the Elliott's eldest son, were on that train, about to begin a new chapter of their lives. One from which I prayed they would return.

The world teetered on the brink of an unimaginable disaster.

My shoulder twinged and an ache I was rarely bothered with these days dredged up grim memories. For Maisie's sake, I quashed them... not today.

I glanced up at the old clock standing proudly on the platform, gleaming in the winter's sunlight. It still kept perfect time, more than half a century since it was crafted. I don't suppose most people noticed it or, if they did, considered it old-fashioned — a remnant of a bygone era. Yet this was where my life changed forever.

I looked down at my beautiful wife. Her glossy hair might be sprinkled with an odd trace of grey, but her face was as youthful as the day we met.

"Come on, love. Standing here won't change anything. How about we go across the way and treat ourselves to coffee and a teacake?"

She tilted her head. Her smile was a trifle wobbly, and her incredible blue-grey eyes brimmed with tears. "You always come up with the best ideas, Fred Cuthbert." She stretched up on tiptoe to brush her lips against mine.

I returned her kiss with fervour, then took her hand.

You never know what might happen... in an innocuous corner of a quiet platform...

...under the clock

About the Author

Rosie Chapel lives in Perth, Australia with her hubby and three furkids. When not writing, she loves catching up with friends, burying herself in a book (or three), discovering the wonders of Western Australia, or — and the best — a quiet evening at home with her husband, enjoying a glass of wine and a movie.

Website: www.rosiechapel.com

Other Books By Rosie Chapel

The Unconventional Duchess

Rescuing Her Knight

Elusive Hearts - *An Unexpected Romance*: Book One

His Fiery Hoyden

A Regency Duet

A Regency Christmas Double

Fate is Curious

A Christmas Prayer *with Ashlee Shades*

The Lady's Wager

Winning Emma

A Love Impossible

Unravelling Roana

Love Kindled

Fairy Tale Romance

Chasing Bluebells

Contemporary Romances

Of Ruins and Romance

All At Once It's You

Cobweb Dreams

Just One Step

His Heart's Second Sigh

Dystopian Romance

Echoes & Illusions *with Rori Bleu*

Historical Fiction/Romance

The Pomegranate Tree

Hannah's Heirloom - Book One

Hoping to trace the origins of an ancient ruby clasp, a gift from her long dead grandmother, Hannah Wilson travels to the fortress of Masada with her best friend, Max. Strange dreams concerning a rebel ambush begin to haunt Hannah and following a tragic accident, she slips into the world of Ancient Masada.

A woman out of time, Hannah must rely on her instincts and her knowledge of what will befall this citadel to survive. Will she escape, or is she doomed to die along with hundreds of others as Masada falls — and what does any of this have to do with an ancient ruby clasp?

Echoes of Stone and Fire

Hannah's Heirloom - Book Two

Pompeii - a vibrant city lost in time following the AD79 eruption of Vesuvius. Now rediscovered, archaeologists yearn for an opportunity to uncover the town's past. Some things, however, are best left alone - revealing the secrets hidden beneath the stones could prove perilous. Hannah and Max are brought to Pompeii by a surprise invitation to join an excavation team who are trying to uncover the city's long history.

After entering an excavated house that bears a Hebrew inscription, Hannah's two worlds collide, and she falls back through time to ancient Pompeii. A place where her ancestor is a physician to gladiators engaged in mortal combat, where riotous mobs run amok and where a ghost from the past returns to haunt her.

Will Hannah and her loved ones manage to escape the devastation she knows is coming, before the town is engulfed in volcanic ash? Will she ever find her way back to Max the love of her life, waiting not so patiently millennia away? Or will echoes be all that remain?

Embers of Destiny

Hannah's Heirloom - Book Three

AD80 - Hannah and Maxentius must embark on a new journey to Northern Britannia. This harsh frontier is far from the comforts of Rome and danger lurks where least expected; a garrison of soldiers, some unhappy with their isolated posting; local tribes, outwardly accepting of their Roman occupier, but who may still resent the seizure of their lands.

Millennia away, Hannah Vallier finds a familiar item while working in a museum near Hadrian's Wall. It is the pomegranate; carved by Maxentius on Masada. Before Hannah can discuss it with Max, disaster strikes! Believing her husband has been killed, Hannah retreats into the past, her soul melding with that of her ancestor, but with little idea of what they could face. Is the risk from the conquered tribes, or much closer to home?

As rebellion threatens to shatter a fragile peace, Hannah's heart whispers that just maybe Max isn't dead and that he is calling her home. Can she trust her heart, or will she remain caught out of time, her destiny floating away like embers on a breeze?

Etched in Starlight

Hannah's Heirloom - Prequel

Maxentius - a Roman soldier fresh from the battlefields of Armenia, arrives to take command of the military outpost of Masada, Herod's isolated citadel in the Judaean desert. A seemingly mundane posting after years of warfare, Maxentius finds it more challenging to maintain a focused garrison than to face the wrath of the Parthians across a disputed frontier.

Hannah - a young Hebrew physician spends her days dealing with injuries from street brawls, deprivation, disease and loss. As her beloved Jerusalem plunges into chaos, her brother — who belongs to a band of rebels determined to drive out their Roman occupiers — tells her of their plans to storm a desert fortress and steal the weapons stored there, persuading his reluctant sister to go with him.

Masada - following the ambush, Hannah finds and treats three badly wounded Roman soldiers. In the aftermath and against impossible odds, Hannah and Maxentius realise that they are more than healer and captive, their fate already etched in starlight.

Prelude to Fate

For Lucia, staring into the jaws of an horrific death, escape seems impossible.

Rufius Atellus, a veteran Roman soldier, is appalled when he recognises one of the victims about to be executed. Surely this is a ghastly mistake?

A ferocious she-wolf, anticipating a tasty meal, suddenly finds herself under a human's control.

In an unexpected twist, and as danger threatens, the lives of all three become inextricably entwined.

Was it chance brought them together in that theatre of bloodshed, or simply a prelude to fate?

Legacy of Flame and Ash

A Hannah's Heirloom Story

An unremarkable family ring — lost when its owner was killed in the catastrophic eruption of Vesuvius — is excavated after nearly two millennia buried under tons of pumice and ash, setting off an extraordinary sequence of events.

A brazen robbery, and the ring is lost again. The theft and subsequent investigation, inspire twelve-year-old Cristiano Rossi to dedicate his life to the search and recovery of stolen artefacts.

Fast forward twenty years. Whispers of a rare item being offered for sale on the black market, initiates a joint operation between the Italian and British branches of the, colloquially named, Art Squad.

Hannah Vallier and her tech savvy assistant, Bryony Emerson — whose abilities to track down the untraceable, led to them assisting the UK Art and Antiquities Unit — have unearthed an intriguing thread. Reluctantly, Cristiano agrees to team up with the pair to thwart the traffickers, retrieve the artefact and, hopefully, dismantle the site.

What ought to be a routine assignment is complicated by a rogue operative, an unexpected romance, an ancient connection, and a *very* angry ghost!

A Guardian Unexpected

The Nettleby Trilogy: Book One

August 1914: Europe is on the brink of catastrophe. In a small village in rural Lincolnshire, a wife kisses her husband goodbye.

Childhood sweethearts, Eliza and Joe have only been married two years. They could not have imagined how soon they would be torn apart by war, nor that the most unexpected of guardians would offer them hope during their darkest hours.

Under the Clock

The Nettleby Trilogy: Book Two

England 1908: Under the clock, on a sleepy station platform nestled in rural Lincolnshire, an unexpected romance blossoms.

Maisie: Every Friday, at precisely five to six, a handsome young man arrives at the station. I know the time because I can see the clock. The train pulls in, punctual as always, and among the alighting passengers is an elderly gentleman. The young man greets him with a smile and a handshake, then tucks his arm through the older man's and they leave the platform.

Every Friday.

Occasionally, we exchange a glance or two and, to be fair, I suspect I notice him more than he notices me.

Fred: I count the hours until Friday afternoon comes around. Not only because this marks the start of the weekend but also, and more importantly, I get to see the flower girl. I am clueless as to her name, yet my heart begins to race the minute the station comes into view. I almost run up the steps onto the platform, hoping for a glimpse of her bright smile.

Every Friday.

I doubt she ever notices me. I'm just a village lad, one more faceless person in the throng.

Then again, you never know what might happen… in an innocuous corner of a quiet platform…

…under the clock

Evie's War

with Rori Bleu

World War II catapulted ordinary people into extraordinary service to save the world from an insidious evil… even if that meant being forced to do things which, under normal circumstances, would be considered abhorrent.

Genevieve Rousseau, Evie to a select few, was one such person who could not escape this fate. Despite her covert endeavours to liberate Paris from the Germans, she finds herself labelled a collaborator and an enemy of the French Republic.

Her only hope of vindication lies in helping a dangerously handsome American, with questionable motives, to uncover the Germans' final revenge.

Could struggling to resist Major Jack Donovon prove to be the decisive battle in Evie's War?

Regency Romance

Once Upon An Earl

Linen and Lace - Book One

When Fate saw fit to intervene in the life of Giles Trevallier, the very respectable Earl of Winchester, by dropping a female — soaked to the skin and with no memory of who she is or how she came to be there — literally at his feet, no one could have predicted the outcome.

While uncovering her identity, Giles realises he is falling hopelessly in love with his mystery guest, who unbeknownst to him, is succumbing to similar emotions; but, when the heart is involved, a thoughtless word or gesture can thwart even Fate's best-laid plans.

Faced with misunderstandings, whispers of scandal, secret documents and foreign agents, their chance at a happy ever after seems elusive, but fairy tales often happen when least expected, and love — however inconvenient — usually finds a way to conquer all.

To Unlock Her Heart

Linen and Lace - Book Two

Abused by a duke, and shunned by Society, relief seems at hand when Grace Aldeburgh is bequeathed a house in a small village, far from malicious gossips.

Once there, a tentative friendship blooms between Grace and Theo Elliott, the local doctor, who has already resolved to be the man to unlock her heart.

Just when happiness appears to be within her grasp, her erstwhile tormentor once again stalks Grace. After a failed kidnap attempt, the duke's quest culminates in an acrimonious confrontation, and the reason for his venal pursuit becomes agonisingly clear.

Love on a Winter's Tide

Linen and Lace - Book Three

Every day, Helena disappears into a world few acknowledge, helping the poor, downtrodden, and abused. A husband is the last thing she can be bothered with.

Busy managing his shipping line, Hugh Drummond sees no need for a wife, whose only joy is dancing and frivolity. If — and it was a huge if — he ever married, it would be to a woman as capable as he, not some giddy society Miss.

Then, Hugh meets Helena and despite their resolve, fate, it seems, has other ideas. As their attraction deepens however, treachery threatens to tear them apart. Will they uncover the perpetrator in time, or will their love be swept away, lost forever on a winter's tide?

A Love Unquenchable

Linen and Lace - Book Four

Jessica Drummond, a bright and cheerful young woman, rarely gives romance, let alone love, a thought. Long hours working in her brother's shipping office affords little chance of her ever meeting an eligible bachelor.

Duncan Barrington, veteran of the Napoleonic Wars, believes himself wounded in both body and soul. He has no intention of inflicting his demons on anyone, certainly not a beautiful and, in his opinion, irresponsible city lady.

One cold and snowy morning, the plight of a bedraggled puppy throws Jessica and Duncan together and, as a spark of something indefinable yet wholly unquenchable begins to burn, it is unclear who rescued whom.

A Hidden Rose

Linen and Lace - Book Five

After witnessing his mother's grief at the loss of his father, Nick Drummond resolved never to cause someone he loved such distress. Even the happiness of his siblings would not sway him — until he met Rose.

Rose Archer was almost content assisting her doctor father in a tiny fishing village in the north of Yorkshire. To experience the world beyond, a tantalising dream — until she met Nick.

Unexpectedly, the impossible becomes possible, and the renounced — desired above all things, but the shipwreck that brought them together, may yet tear them apart. Will Nick learn to trust his heart, or will his love for Rose remain forever hidden

The Daffodil Garden

Horrifically scarred during the war, William Harcourt - Marquis of Blackthorne - prefers to spend his days in the quiet of his daffodil garden; plants do not pity, turn away, or judge.

Lucy Truscott, whose life is far removed from that of the *ton*, has no idea that by saving the life of a young woman, to whom she bears an uncanny resemblance, her own will be placed in mortal danger.

A chance encounter leads to something more. William begins to trust that Lucy sees the man beneath the scars, while Lucy is persuaded that love might actually transcend status.

Unfortunately, before their courtship has really begun, someone has every intention of ending it - permanently.

The Unconventional Duchess

Refusing to suffer the humiliation of her husband flaunting his mistress at Society events, the newly married Duchess of Wallingstead, Ella Lennox, takes control of her life. She leaves London for the family's country seat in remote Yorkshire.

A woman alone, Ella spends the next four years turning a cold, grim house into a home, and transforming the fortunes of the estate. Not afraid of hard work, she soon earns the respect of those around her with her determination and unconventional attitude.

Out of the blue, the duke arrives. Resigned to another arduous visit, Ella is stunned when it seems he is attempting to court her.

Impossible!

Could her dream of a happy marriage be about to come true?

Everything hangs on a snowstorm, a herd of cows and an uninvited guest!

Rescuing Her Knight

The *de Wiltons* — Book One

A story, invented to keep a little girl distracted, marks the beginning of another tale. One destined to remain unfinished for twenty years.

At thirteen, Adam Marchmain became Kitty de Wilton's 'Knight of the Garden' — a title bestowed following an accident which resulted in six-year-old Kitty having her knee sutured. Kitty never forgot his gallantry, but pledges made as children rarely survive into adulthood.

Their paths separated until Fate decreed, they meet again.

Widowed, badly disfigured and his sight ruined, Adam returns to his family home, a shadow of his former self.

Similarly afflicted, although her scars are invisible, Kitty — against her better judgement — is persuaded to help Adam banish his demons. This requires a subterfuge which, if discovered, might shatter more than the bonds of friendship forged two decades previously.

To Kitty, determined to break through the shield Adam has erected, the risk is worth it.

To see his smile and hear his laughter.

To rescue the knight of her childhood.

Just when a fairy tale ending is within her grasp, Kitty is threatened by the man who murdered her husband. In a cruel twist the tables are turned, and Kitty is the one who needs rescuing.

Elusive Hearts

An Unexpected Romance — Book One

What happens when two people whose elusive hearts fight an indefinable attraction, neither looked for nor desired, dare to dream?

When her fiancé and sister abscond to Gretna Green on her wedding day, Sapphira Beresford longs to escape, to avoid the gossipmongers gloating over her misfortune. Disillusioned, she is determined not to be burnt again, swearing off romance and marriage.

A fortuitous invitation sees her embarking on a journey to Pompeii where she meets Leofwin Colleville, reclusive marquis, amateur antiquarian, and her host for the duration.

Although enamoured of the ruins gradually being unearthed and ecstatic to have the opportunity to assist, Sapphira is troubled by her host's attitude, which blows hot and cold.

A confirmed bachelor, Leofwin Colleville is happiest surrounded by ancient ruins, and would prefer to brave the whole of Napoleon's armies alone, than face a lady on the hunt for a husband. The arrival of an unexpected guest throws his unencumbered existence into turmoil, but the harder he strives to maintain his distance, the more she gets under his skin.

Sparks fly and, as Leofwin's truculence undermines Sapphira's already battered confidence, her adventure of a lifetime seems doomed to disaster.

Until the day she runs afoul of greedy treasure hunters.

In the aftermath what was scorned becomes the one thing they crave above all else, but when it comes to the heart, nothing is ever simple.

His Fiery Hoyden

A Novella

Livvy has no respect for the nobility; they let her down when she most needed them. Why should she accede to their demands now?

Philip, Lord Harrington, is stunned to discover the young heir to the dukedom lives a stone's throw away in a ramshackle cottage, and resolves to restore the child to his birthright.

They meet in a clash of wills, but just when it seems Livvy might surrender, the victory Philip desires, may not taste all that sweet.

A Regency Duet

Luck be a Pirate

Luck wasn't something retired pirate Kennet Alexson believed in — good or bad. However, even he had to concede that landing a job at Trentams shipyard, and meeting Lynette Collins, was more than coincidence.

Fortune it seemed, was smiling on him for once.

As Kennet adjusts to life on dry land, his friendship with Lynette deepens into something far more enduring, and what once seemed elusive now becomes possible.

Unfortunately, fate has other plans, and Kennet's good luck is about to run out.

The Highwayman's Kiss

Surrendered Hearts — Book One

Nothing exciting had ever happened to Juliette St Clair. Her days were spent assisting her father or calling on friends, wandering art galleries, taking constitutionals or, and more preferably, escaping into her books. Her evenings her evenings — an endless round of balls, where she preferred to remain invisible.

Until the day she was robbed by a highwayman.

A Regency Christmas Double

Heart Rescued

Four years since Jasper lost the woman he was hoping to marry. Four years since he closed his heart and withdrew from Society. He has no idea his reclusive existence is about to be shattered.

Enter his sister's best friend, Harriet, a flame haired beauty, who needs his help.

Reluctantly he agrees and as they spend time together, it is clear their feelings run deep. Although Harriet affects Jasper in a way no woman ever has, he believes her to be out of his league ~ but it's Christmas and she might just be the one to melt his frozen heart

Catch a Snowflake

Romance often blossoms in the most unlikely of places - but in a ward full of wounded soldiers - surely not?

When Lucas Withers comes face to face with Jemima Parsons - a young woman who blames him for her brother's injury - falling in love is the last thing on their minds. What neither of them anticipated, was the magic of snowflakes.

Fate is Curious

A Novella

Happily, ever after? No such thing! Bereft, following her beloved husband's sudden death, Lady Charlotte Sherbrooke has lost her belief in romantic nonsense.

Successful shipping merchant, Zacharie Romain, is no stranger to loss; his business can be hazardous. Moreover, his wife died in childbirth and even though it happened a decade ago, he has no mind to expose himself to such sorrow again.

They meet in less than joyful circumstances but, as the year turns and grief diminishes, the woes of a small boy become the catalyst for something wholly unexpected. Can Charlotte and Zacharie trust what Fate has in store or will past heartbreak prevent them from taking a chance on love?

A Christmas Prayer

with Ashlee Shades

A Short Story

An entreaty from a frightened child.

Orphaned and only nine, Caroline Thorne has to grow up before her time. She is doing everything she can to keep what is left of her family together and out of the workhouse but is terrified her prayers are not being heard. Or maybe they are…

A petition from a woman desperate for a family.

A chance meeting with three orphaned siblings, tugs at Elizabeth Barrington's heart strings. Thus far, she and her husband have not been blessed with children and, as Christmas approaches, a plan begins to form - one which might just be the answer to her prayers.

Two Christmas prayers, as different as they are the same.

Will they hear and, more importantly, heed the answer?

The Lady's Wager

Surrendered Hearts- Book Two

A Novelette

Ged Mowbray will do anything to avoid being married off to the suitable prospects his parents insist on parading in front of him.

Melissa Bouchard is under no illusion her sizeable dowry is the attraction to suitors, not her.

An overheard conversation leads to an offer too good to refuse, but what happens when a lady's wager, becomes a gamble on the happily ever after, you did not even realise you wanted?

Winning Emma

Surrendered Hearts - Book Three

A Novelette

Randolph Craythorpe — earl, covert operative, and occasional highwayman — believed his dalliance with Lady Felicity Hartwich would lead to marriage. It did, but not to him! The arrival of an unwelcome guest, however, provides the perfect opportunity to indulge in a little retaliation.

Emma Newbury accompanies her cousin, Lady Charity Anscombe, to London for the Christmas season. Once there, she comes face to face with the three men who witnessed the humiliating aftermath of her father's disgrace — one of whom, to her irritation, has taken up residence in her dreams.

Their infrequent encounters only serve to confuse but, while winter tightens its grip on the city, what was inconceivable becomes the one thing for which they both yearn, yet bound by Society's rules, cannot admit.

As the snow falls, Randolph begins to understand that to win Emma, he will have to surrender.

A Love Impossible

A Regency M/M Novelette

Tasked with investigating a heinous crime, Edward Lindsay travels from London to Dublin — a city which holds too many memories — in the guise of guardian to his sister. He knew it could be hazardous, and relished the challenge, but that wasn't what caused his stomach to tighten as they approached landfall.

Dublin held more than just a murderer.

There was also Aidan.

While attending a party, Aidan Griffen is astonished when he comes face to face with a man who fled Dublin two years previously. A man he has desperately tried to forget.

As Edward closes in on his quarry, a fire, deliberately extinguished, is rekindled. But what of it? Edward and Aidan share a love impossible, and to acknowledge their feelings — more dangerous than confronting a killer.

Is there any hope of a happily ever after?

Unravelling Roana

A Regency Novelette

Tired of being ignored by her husband, Roana Dumont, Countess of Brooketon does the one thing guaranteed to get his attention. She runs away… to Venice, leaving behind a set of riddles for him to solve… *if* he feels their marriage is worth saving.

Gideon Dumont, 6th Earl of Brooketon is flabbergasted when he discovers his wife has apparently vanished off the face of the earth. A series of puzzles, the only clue as to her whereabouts.

The question is… will he unravel them?

Love Kindled

A Regency Novelette

Recently widowed, Amelia Ingram - Countess of Gresham, decides to shake off the fetters from her arranged and loveless marriage. Exploiting her new-found independence, Amelia indulges her yearning to explore - incognito.

Her ploy works so well, she receives an offer of employment from the dangerously handsome, Rupert Latimer - Earl of Badlesmere. On impulse, she accepts and finds herself governess to Cate, a delightful scamp of a child. What began as a bit of a game on Amelia's part, evolves into something far more profound, and a flame she presumed impossible to ignite, is kindled.

An unexpected turn of events leads to yet another offer. This time there is far more at stake and, determined history not repeat itself, Amelia confesses her ruse.

Rupert has been burnt once. Will he douse the spark, or take a risk and trust his heart?

Fairy Tale Romance

Chasing Bluebells

A Fairy Tale Novella

Once upon a time, somewhere in France, there was a man whose reckless obsession led him down a dark path — one which, ultimately, cost him his life. That ought to have been the end of it. Regrettably, as is so often the case, those who least deserve it, suffer for the actions of others.

A decade after being sent away, Sebastien Daviau returns to the little village where everything began. Hoping to lay the ghosts of his childhood to rest, he studiously ignores the possibility, he might run into Charlotte de Montbeliard.

As luck would have it, Charlotte is the one who runs into him… well, his horse… and although the brief encounter leaves a lasting impression, neither recognises the other.

A name revealed causes a freak accident, catapulting Sebastien's past into his present, and bringing him face to face with a man whose reputation would intimidate the most ardent of suitors.

Can whatever is blossoming between Charlotte and Sebastien survive the challenge imposed, or is their happily ever after about to fade as quickly as the bluebells they loved to chase?

Contemporary Romance

Of Ruins and Romance

Kassandra Winters has intrigued Gabriel St Germain since he accidentally knocked her flying outside her university professor's office. Her face haunts his dreams, yet he never expected to see her again. So, he is surprised when she appears, as though destined to do so, in the middle of a ruin, and he concocts a plan to win her heart.

Gabriel's old-fashioned courtship touches something deep inside Kassie and, although struggling to believe someone as handsome as Gabriel could possibly be interested in her, she soon realises she has fallen irrevocably in love with him. However, just as Kassie shares everything of herself with Gabriel, her world comes crashing down.

Can their romance survive, or will it fall in ruins, like the relics of antiquity that brought them together?

All At Once It's You

When Alex arrives in the small village of Rosedale Abbey, to take up a position as a research assistant for a renowned archaeologist, the last thing she is looking for, or expects to find, is love.

Jake was perfectly happy with the status quo. When it came to relationships, he didn't do committed or long term. He called the shots, and if his current flame didn't like it, she knew what to do. A philosophy, which served him well - until he met Alex.

Romance blooms, but even as the untamed wilderness of the North Yorkshire moors weaves its spell, a long-buried secret might yet jeopardise their happily ever after.

Cobweb Dreams

A Novella

A holiday on the Scottish isle of Mull was just the break Chloe Shepherd needed, an escape from her boring office job and her complete lack of anything resembling a social life. Romance, it seems, isn't on the cards and, although Chloe dreams of finding her soulmate she is beginning to believe love is like cobwebs — spun overnight, only to vanish in the early morning breeze.

Under sufferance, Dominic Winters makes a flying visit to Mull to check on a rental property owned by his family. He hasn't got time for this — so indulging in a holiday fling is the last thing on his mind.

A lamb stuck in a bog proves a most unexpected matchmaker and, while Mull weaves its magic, Chloe wonders whether those fragile cobwebs might be far more stubborn than she thought.

Just One Step

A Short Story

In the aftermath of an horrific car accident, Daisy Forrester travels to Italy - hoping, so far from her memories, she might begin to heal.

Archaeologist, and single father, Adam Willoughby is too busy looking after his young daughter to give romance let alone love, a thought.

Neither expects a chance encounter in an ancient ruin to be anything more, but sometimes, that's all it takes.

His Heart's Second Sigh

A Novella

Reuben Faulkner and Paige Latimer are two happily single people,
who have no desire to upset the status quo.

Unexpectedly, they are thrown together, only to discover both want
far more than a casual friendship.

Just when things take an interesting turn, Reuben's past catches up
with them, and threatens to derail their blossoming romance before
it has chance to start.

Dystopian Romance

Echoes & Illusions

The Hunters - Book 1

Twenty years after a global plague, the remnants of civilisation struggle to eke out an existence in a world where humanity is secondary to survival.

On the outskirts of a once vibrant Rome, Gabriel tends his vineyard. From dawn to dusk, he strives to carve out a living, while caring for Bianca, his heavily pregnant wife.

Life might be tough, but at least he had an income, meagre though it was. Trouble seemed a distant memory, until the day he notices their neighbours are not at work in the adjacent fields.

A gruesome discovery sparks a chain of events to rival the conflicts Rome witnessed at the height of its power. Gabriel and Bianca must pit their wits and their lives against a formidable opponent, in an attempt prevent an atrocity none could have predicted.

A bond, forged in a snowy field and strengthened in a city under siege, is put to the ultimate test.

In a world of echoes and illusions, is their love strong enough to surmount the odds, or will it crumble to dust like the empire their enemies are striving to replicate?

www.ingramcontent.com/pod-product-compliance
Lightning Source LLC
Chambersburg PA
CBHW072146130726
47909CB00004BB/1248